BARBARA COMYNS

was born at Bidford-on-Avon, Warwickshire, in 1909. She was mainly educated by governesses until she went to art schools in Stratford-on-Avon and London. She has worked in an advertising agency, a typewriting bureau, dealt in old cars and antique furniture, bred poodles, converted and let flats and has exhibited pictures in The London Group. She was married first in 1931, to an artist, and for the second time in 1945. She and her second husband lived in Spain for eighteen years.

She started writing fiction at the age of ten and her first novel, *Sisters by a River*, was published in 1947. Since then she has published seven novels: *Our Spoons Came From Woolworths* (1950), *Who was Changed and Who was Dead* (1955), *The Vet's Daughter* (1959), *The Skin Chairs* (1962), *Birds in Tiny Cages* (1964), *A Touch of Mistletoe* (1967) and *The Juniper Tree* (1985). She is also the author of *Out of the Red into the Blue* (1960) which describes her time in Spain. *The Vet's Daughter* is her best-known novel, and has been both serialized and dramatised by BBC Radio; it was also turned into a musical called *The Clapham Wonder* by Sandy Wilson of 'The Boy Friend' fame. Barbara Comyns has one son, one daughter, seven grandchildren and one great grandchild. She lives in Twickenham, Middlesex.

Virago publishes *Our Spoons Came From Woolworths*, *The Vet's Daughter*, *Sisters by a River*, *The Skin Chairs* and *Who was Changed and Who was Dead*.

BARBARA COMYNS

WHO WAS CHANGED AND WHO WAS DEAD

WITH A NEW INTRODUCTION BY
URSULA HOLDEN

PENGUIN BOOKS – VIRAGO PRESS

Penguin Books
Viking Penguin Inc., 40 West 23rd Street,
New York, New York 10010, U.S.A.
Penguin Books Ltd, Harmondsworth,
Middlesex, England
Penguin Books Australia Ltd, Ringwood,
Victoria, Australia
Penguin Books Canada Limited, 2801 John Street,
Markham, Ontario, Canada L3R 1B4
Penguin Books (N.Z.) Ltd, 182–190 Wairau Road,
Auckland 10, New Zealand

First published in Great Britain by The Bodley Head 1954

This edition first published in Great Britain by Virago Press Limited 1987

Published in Penguin Books 1987

Copyright Barbara Comyns, 1954
Introduction copyright © Ursula Holden, 1987
All rights reserved.

Printed in Great Britain
by Anchor Brendon Ltd. of Tiptree, Essex

Of what has been and might have been
And who was changed and who was dead

LONGFELLOW

INTRODUCTION

Who was Changed and Who was Dead was first published in 1954 and was Barbara Comyns' third novel. A few critics were sufficiently percipient to concede that it was indeed the little masterpiece that the publisher (Bodley Head) claimed, but there were those who condemned it as being too unpleasant to stomach. Barbara Comyns was accused of wallowing in repulsiveness. The book was banned in Ireland under the Censorship of Publications Act. Presumably this was for its power to disgust rather than for reasons of blasphemy or obscenity. Barbara Comyns' ruthless eye defies squeamishness; nothing is too raw for her consideration.

Once more she deals with the complexities of family life, an area in which she excels. It is 1914 in a Warwickshire village (the county where she herself was born) which is stricken first by flood, then plague. Emma, Hattie and Dennis, the children of Ebin Willoweed, are terrorised by their grandmother who tries to rule the village too. As in *Sisters by a River* (1947) the river influences their lives. From the opening page where it has burst its banks and flooded the family home Barbara Comyns spares nothing; no detail is too forbidding: "A passing pig squealing, its short legs madly beating the water and tearing at its throat, which was red and bleeding. . ."

The maids, Norah and Eunice, repair the flood damage and laugh as they chase a floating basket filled with eggs. Mirth turns to alarm as a large shadow passes the window. The last of the peacocks is flying to the coalshed roof. The peacock is an omen. The other peacocks are drowned, their bodies float around the garden. Broody hens continue to sit on their eggs until they are covered in water. They squawk as the water rises; their red combs disappear. Old Ives the handyman is clearing up.

"Don't go yet, boy! Look at this little puss I found," and he produced a dead, sodden kitten from his pocket, the ginger fur had come away from its tail and the bone was exposed.

Barbara Comyns deftly balances savagery with innocence, depravity with lyric interludes. The grandmother has a forked tongue and berates the gentle Emma who combs her marmalade-coloured hair and longs wistfully for a better life. She remembers a bee the size of a lemon that she once saw, and which no one believed in, saying it must have been a bird.

She felt overcome with a longing for beautiful clothes and an admirer, or several admirers; overcome with a longing to travel, perhaps even in a private yacht. She imagined a white one gliding through impossibly blue water, and saw herself on deck wearing an evening gown with a train. And then there was the tango. How beautiful it would be to tango to exotic music, and perhaps go to something called a tango tea!

But Emma is resigned, nothing like that will happen to her. No dances, no admirers: she will go on being herself and nothing will happen at all.

Her younger sister Hattie is a half black child. She is the cheerful one of the family, sitting splashing her dark feet happily in the flood water in the dining room. The grandmother hits out at her woolly head. The colour of Hattie's skin is unremarked and causes no surprise. Her father, Ebin, prefers her because "she is so jolly . . . always game for anything, much the best of the lot". He wonders casually how on earth his deceased wife could have found a black lover in their lonely village. Emma, in his opinion, is as "damn queer as her mother" and his son Dennis is a cissy.

> "He's so damn nervous he drives me crazy. Of course he needs to go to school; but the old woman is so bloody mean she'd never pay the fees. There are not many men who would spend hours teaching their children like I do."

Barbara Comyns writes of mysterious or disadvantaged children elsewhere. In *Sisters by a River* there is a child who "I shall never mention because I know they [sic] would hate to appear in it". In *The Skin Chairs* there is a child without a hand. *The Juniper Tree* has another half black child. In her fiction the children are accepted without surprise or prejudice.

The flooding river is a foretaste of worse misfortune. The poisoned bread sold by the village baker claims its victims. Barbara Comyns says that the idea came to her when she read a newspaper report of the fearful outbreak of ergot poisoning that happened in the French village of Pont d'Esprit in August 1951. She researched the subject in medical journals and the story of *Who was Changed and Who was Dead* then came to her comparatively easily. The book is totally unbiographical. She let her imagination take over.

Contrary to the belief that writing reflects the writer's state of mind, Barbara Comyns was not unhappy when she wrote this troubled book. This was a trouble-free time in her life, when she and her family lived in South Kensington. Her husband and children were out during the day; she had time for writing and everything was going well. This is the only book that she allowed her family to see before it was finished. As with most writers, her rule of secrecy is strict. Nothing must be told; creative ideas must not be put at risk or they might vanish. While writing the book ideas for *The Vet's Daughter* were already coming to her, almost as if the way was being prepared. That *Who was Changed and Who was Dead* was received with less enthusiasm than her previous two novels (*Sisters by a River* and *Our Spoons Came from Woolworths*, 1950), was a disappointment to Barbara Comyns but she went on to write *The Vet's Daughter* (1959).

The characters of *Who was Changed and Who was Dead* are cleverly crafted, innocence blending with dismay.

> "Please God, don't let her be in one of her rages," prayed Emma . . . Grandmother Willoweed was pouring herself a glass of port. Both ends of her tongue were protruding—rather a bad sign . . . 'Doctor Hatt was called away in the middle of my whist drive. His wife was worse—her nose was bleeding.' She filled her glass from the decanter and gave Emma a strange glance.
>
> "Well, peoples' noses are always bleeding. You are supposed to put a large key down their back." . . .
>
> "Well, my dear, a key wouldn't have been much use in this case; this was a peculiar kind of nosebleed. It went on and on until the bed became filled with blood—at least that is what I heard—it went on and on and the mattress was soaked and the floor became crimson; it went on and on until Mrs Hatt died."
>
> She took another sip of port.
>
> "Yes, Mrs Hatt is dead now."

Emma sadly remembers Mrs Hatt's comfortable figure and the brown plaits twisted round her head. What would become

of the marmalade she had helped her make last spring? Could
you eat dead people's marmalade? And the Christmas puddings
hanging in Mrs Hatt's kitchen; how could Dr Hatt "have a
merry Christmas eating his dead wife's pudding while she was
lying so cold in the churchyard"?

Such ponderings reveal Emma's caring heart.

Meanwhile, Old Ives in the potting shed weaves a wreath for
Mrs Hatt's grave—

> full bloom roses because she was a full blown woman, although she
> had never had a child. Ives liked to choose suitable flowers for his
> wreathes. He often planned the one he would make for Grand-
> mother Willoweed:—thistles and hogswart and grey-green
> holly—sometimes he would grant her one yellow dandelion. Ebin
> was to have one of bindweed and tobacco plants. Quite often
> people would die when the flowers already chosen for them were
> not in season. Then he made a temporary wreath for them, and
> months later they received the real one.

The other characters show a touching tenderness towards
each other. Norah and Eunice, having changed from their
morning print dresses into black afternoon uniform, sit in their
window with their arms round each other until it is time to start
the tea. Though death and descriptions of death abound in all
Barbara Comyns' work, everyone appears to enjoy the funerals
and the flowers. In *The Skin Chairs* the children make delicate
wreaths for the graves of baby chickens. Only the grandmother
remains bad tempered and vituperative to the end, her black
clothes, her forked tongue and lizard-like eyes a symbol of the
evil that poisons the village.

But calm and glimpses of peace lighten the dark, often seen·
through the gentle eyes of Emma.

She was alone except for a swan and its family of cygnets. The swan gently passed. There were fields on either side of the river. Some were freshly green where the hay had already been cut, and one was all sparkling blue with early cabbages. In a small bay a group of cows stood knee-deep in the water and gracefully turned their heads to watch her as she passed. She came to a little wrecked pleasure-steamer, which had become embedded in the mud several summers ago and which no one had bothered to remove. It had been a vulgar, tubby little boat when it used to steam through the water with its handful of holiday-makers, giving shrill whistles at every bend and causing a wash that disturbed the fishermen as they sat peacefully on the banks; but, now it lay sideways in the mud with its gaudy paint all bleached, it was almost beautiful.

It is Emma who mothers Hattie and Dennis, providing them with the security that they fail to receive from their monstrous and greedy grandmother or their self-absorbed father. Emma takes the younger ones on river picnics and they are secure in their sealed childhood world.

When the girls tired of rowing they tied the boat up under a willow tree. It seemed as if they were in a green tent. They sat there for a little time; but the bottom of the boat smelt of fish, so they climbed out and lay on the river bank in the sun. The river breeze rustled the rushes and made a whispering sound. After a time Emma opened the picnic basket and they ate honey sandwiches with ants on them and drank the queer tea that always comes from a thermos. When there was no more picnic fare left they lay in the sun again in a straight line, and became very warm and watched dragon-flies. Some were light blue, small and elegant; others were a shining green; and there were enormous stripey ones that took large bites out of the water-lily leaves.

Serenity never lasts very long. Madness and savagery resulting from eating the poisoned bread take their toll. The crowds outside Old Toby's cottage are reminiscent of the crowds that witness Alice Rowland's death in *The Vet's Daughter*. Barbara Comyns handles bloodthirsty hysteria as deftly as she handles idyllic harmony.

Emma and Dennis cringed against a hedge. Besides the shouting there were other most disturbing sounds like some great malevolent animal snorting and grunting, and there was a stench of evilness and sweating, angry bodies. A man with his shirt all hanging out pushed past Emma, and in the moonlight she could see his face all terrible, with loose lips snarling and saliva pouring down his chin. Shrieks of laughter greeted him when he climbed on the thatched roof and shouted and swore down the chimney. Several men carried lanterns, which they wildly waved above their heads and which made a strange and dancing light. Emma and Dennis crept against the hedge, and, although they were pushed and jostled, they clung to each other and were not parted. They stumbled over two unheeding figures rolling and grunting on the grass, and a woman with her mouth all bleeding pushed them out of her way as she ran yelling towards the village.

The final description of Old Toby's dying body crawling from his burning cottage is pure Grand Guignol. We can smell the burning flesh and smouldering cloth. We can feel Emma's distress. "He smelt so dreadful, and he crawled..." The grandmother gets her desserts. Change or death is the outcome. The poisoning is a hideous catharsis that leaves the remaining characters happier, with more assured futures. Little dark-skinned Hattie weeps over her brother's bowl of grass that he treasured. She cuts it with nail scissors. Children have short memories and horrors recede.

The book has triumphed in the face of time. Barbara Comyns would not now be accused of wallowing in unpleasantness; our reactions have become more subdued and we are less squeamish. The censorship in Ireland has lost its bite.

Barbara Comyns was also a painter of some distinction and she exhibited at the London Group which showed the Vorticists. These painters set out to jolt complacency, and this is what Barbara Comyns does in this book. Yet running throughout is a vein of poetry and compassion that pities and pardons the behaviour of those it describes. It can be read as a fairy tale, an allegory or the chronicle of extraordinary events in the life of a country family. Few would dispute that it is a little masterpiece as well as being an imaginative *tour de force*.

Ursula Holden, London, 1986.

Time:

SUMMER ABOUT SEVENTY YEARS AGO

Place:

WARWICKSHIRE

CHAPTER I

THE DUCKS swam through the drawing-room windows. The weight of the water had forced the windows open; so the ducks swam in. Round the room they sailed quacking their approval; then they sailed out again to explore the wonderful new world that had come in the night. Old Ives stood on the verandah steps beating his red bucket with a stick while he called to them, but today they ignored him and floated away white and shining towards the tennis court. Swans were there, their long necks excavating under the dark, muddy water. All around there was a wheezy creaking noise as the water soaked into unaccustomed places, and in the distance a roar and above it the shouts of men trying to rescue animals from the low-lying fields. A passing pig squealing, its short legs madly beating the water and tearing at its throat, which was red and bleeding, and a large flat-bottomed boat followed with men inside. The boat whirled round and round in the fierce current; but eventually the pig was saved, and squealed even louder. The children,

I

Hattie and Dennis, watched the rescue from a bedroom window, and suddenly the sun came out very
bright and strong and everywhere became silver.
Old Ives below said, "It's a bad thing for the sun to
shine on a flood, it draws the dampness back to the
sky." The grandmother came and joined him, and
they talked together in the verandah. There was a
great smell of mud, and it was the first of June.

In the kitchens the maids pinned their skirts
up high and splashed about in the water trying
to prepare breakfast. Their bare legs became quite
red. In the large range a fire burnt brightly, and the
flames were reflected in the water, but there was a
smell of damp and cellars all around. The girls—
they were sisters called Norah and Eunice—laughed
as they chased a floating basket filled with eggs.
Their laughter changed to screeches when a huge, crying shadow passed the window; but it was only the
last of the peacocks flying from a tree to the coalshed
roof. The other three peacocks had been drowned in
the night, and their bodies were floating sadly round
the garden; but no one knew this yet, or what had
happened to the hens. As the day went on the hens,
locked in their black shed, became depressed and
hungry and one by one they fell from their perches
and committed suicide in the dank water below, leaving only the cocks alive. The sorrowful sitting hens, all
broody, were in another dark, evil-smelling shed
and they died too. They sat on their eggs in a black
broody dream until they were covered in water.
They squarked a little; but that was all. For a few

moments just their red combs were visible above the water, and then they disappeared.

Ebin Willoweed rowed his daughters round the sub-merged garden. He rowed with gentle ineffectual strokes because he was a slothful man, but a strong vein of inquisitiveness kept him from being entirely indolent. He rowed away under a blazing sun; the light was very bright and the water brilliant. Some-times there would be a bumping and scraping under the boat as it passed over a garden seat or tree trunk or some object only slightly covered by water. Strange objects of pitiful aspect floated past: the bloated body of a drowned sheep, the wool wither-ing about in the water, a white bee-hive with the per-plexed bees still around; a new-born pig, all pink and dead; and the mournful bodies of the peacocks. It seemed so stark to see such sorrowful things under the blazing sun and blue sky—a mist of rain would have been more fitting. Now a tabby cat with a distended belly passed, its little paws showing above the water, its small head hanging low. Ebin Willoweed turned his round blue eyes in its direction with interest and poked at it with his oar. His daughters were filled with sadness and asked to be taken back to the house, but he turned the boat towards the river. Then the cur-rent became much stronger and there was the sound of swirling water against trees and posts and he had to get one of the girls to take an oar to get the boat back to the safety of the garden. After this exertion he became quite agreeable to returning to the house.

When they entered the house the grandmother ran

down from her bedroom to meet them. She splashed into the watery hall, and cried in her deep, rather nasal voice. "Tell me all about the flood. Has the bridge been damaged? Is the weir still standing? Has anyone been drowned, do you know?" She bombarded them with questions. With one hand she held up her long black skirts; with the other she clutched her large curved ear trumpet. Emma, the eldest grand-daughter, took the trumpet and shouted down it for a few moments. It became filled with beads of moisture, and she handed it back to her grandmother and wiped her mouth on her cotton skirt. The grandmother cried, "Don't go yet, tell me more. What about my rose beds?" Her son seized the trumpet she was wildly waving above her head and shouted down its black depths, "Dead animals floating everywhere. Your roses are completely covered, you will be lucky if you get a bunch."

"Lunch, lunch, what about lunch! Is it ready?" The old lady waded into the dining-room where Dennis was amusing himself floating a fleet of toy boats.

"Hallo, landlubber!" his father greeted him. The boy didn't answer, but bent down to float the boat he was holding. His ears became red.

"Would you like to come out with me and rescue a few sheep?" his father asked in a tone of forced heartiness.

"No thank you, father. I think I feel rather sick today."

His father looked at him with impatient disgust.

"Christ! Don't you ever want to do anything, you

little cissy? Oh well, I'll go up to my room; it's the only comfortable place today. No newspapers, I suppose."

He left the room still grumbling and mounted the stairs to his den at the top of the house.

"Anyone might feel sick," the small boy said to himself, and went on playing with his boats. He had made them himself and they were his great pride.

"Don't mind father," said Hattie. "Have you realized this flood will put our lessons out of father's mind for days, perhaps even a week?" She laughed happily and began to splash about in the water with her dark bare feet. The grandmother observed there were no signs of lunch and that she was being unnecessarily splashed, so she hit Hattie on her woolly head and said, "Stop doing that, child. Go into the kitchen and see what those lazy trollops are up to," and Hattie went off bawling down the passage.

Upstairs Emma sat on her bedroom window-sill. The casement windows were wide open and she basked in the sun and combed her marmalade-coloured hair. She closed her eyes and forgot the sad, drowned sights of the morning. A feeling of deep satisfaction came over her as she felt the warmth of the sun and combed her hair, dreamily. Then she opened her eyes and examined her hands and pinched her nails at the tip, hoping they would become long and pointed.

"Oh, how I would love to go to a dance and wear a real evening dress," she thought, "but nothing like that will happen—no dances, no admirers. I shall just be me, and nothing will happen at all."

In his den above, her father sat in his shabby leather armchair and wondered if he had been rather hard on Dennis.

"Poor little wretch," he thought, "he's so damn nervous he drives me crazy. Of course he needs to go to school; but the old woman is so bloody mean she'd never pay the fees. There are not many men who would spend hours teaching their children like I do. People say I'm lazy but it takes a lot of energy to do a thing like that."

He lit his pipe.

"It's a good idea to smoke a pipe, then people don't expect you to keep offering them cigarettes. I once knew a little nurse, she was a sweet little thing, but smoked like hell and expected me to provide the cigarettes. I had to give her up in the end; it was too expensive. I think that's what started me on a pipe."

He relit it.

"I like this room. People can laugh at it; but it's jolly comfortable."

He walked across the room to the shabby old cottage piano. Some of the ivories were missing and the ones that remained were yellow. He stood strumming for a few moments, then sat on the round plush stool and played some rather rollicking music which appeared to cheer him up quite considerably. Then his eyes fell on the mantlepiece. It was draped with dark green velvet, complete with pom-poms, and on it were a half-empty bottle of beer and a dirty glass with a few dead flies floating about. He emptied the flies into the overflowing ash tray, and poured out a glass of beer. It was rather flat but not undrinkable. As he drank it, rocking backwards and forwards on his toes, he said to himself:

"After lunch I'll go out in the boat again; I might see something interesting. There should be a lot of interesting things around after a flood like this. Surely in all this water someone must have drowned. I'll take Hattie with me; she's always game for anything. Emma's strange, damn queer like her mother; but Hattie is so jolly, much the best of the lot. Of course she isn't my child, I don't believe in all that village nonsense about her being black because Jenny died before she was born; it's just an old wives' tale. The blackness didn't notice so much when she was born; but it's unmistakeable now. How on earth Jenny found a black lover here, in this lonely village, that is what beats me."

There was a great booming of the gong and his thoughts became disturbed; so he hurriedly finished his stale beer and went downstairs, where he found his family having lunch in the old nursery, which was comparatively dry. It was some years since he had been in the room. It was very dark with fir trees pushing in at the window. It had been his nursery when he was a child, and he was amused to see the wallpaper and furniture still the same, and the bow-fronted chest of drawers, the scrap-book screen, the old red couch with the springs hanging down below, and the tallboy which had got him into trouble because he kept frogs in the top drawer. He looked round the room with great satisfaction, and ate his gammon and green peas with his family around him, and felt content.

As the day went on the flood began to subside. It left the Willoweeds' house, and in its place was mud and river weed and a deep smell of dampness. The children set stones in the garden to mark the flood's retreat. The garden sloped down to the river and by the evening half of it was visible again, the flowers lying wet and heavy on the ground, the grass a verdant green. A few strange dead objects lay about. Old Ives collected them and put them in the stokehole. Dennis sadly watched him pushing in a peacock.

"Are you sure it's dead, Old Ives?" he asked.

"Of course the poor bugger's dead," he muttered, and slammed the door on it. The remaining peacock began to screech. There was thunder in the air, and the sky had become yellow and grey.

"There, I said it would rain, and rain it will," said the old man. "That peacock don't half hum. It must be the feathers burning."

He opened the stokehole door a chink and a great smoke and stench came out. Dennis said:

"I think it's time I went to bed now. Good night, Old Ives, I'm glad your ducks came back."

"Don't go yet, boy! Look at this little puss I found," and he produced a dead, sodden kitten from his pocket, the ginger fur had come away from its tail and the bone was exposed. Dennis had gone; so the kitten followed the peacock into the stokehole.

During the night the storm broke. The grandmother woke the children and maids who were sleeping quite peacefully.

"The house will be struck. Come to the cellars!" she cried, "Come to the cellars!"

The children were dragged down to the cellars which were completely filled with water, and everyone became very wet. Then they were herded into the large stone kitchen, and sat shivering and crying under the kitchen table.

"Pull the curtains, you fools!" screamed the grandmother as a flash of blue lightning filled the kitchen. Norah climbed onto the table to reach the window; but a great clap of thunder came, and she made a dash to the broom-cupboard under the stairs.

Grandmother Willoweed yelled, "Coward! What do you think I pay you for, you insubordinate slut?"

There was another flash, more yells and cries and a tearing clap of thunder. In the midst of it Ebin Willoweed appeared on the back stairs holding a candle. He saw his mother crouching under the table with the children. Emma remained upstairs. Eunice had joined her sister in the broom cupboard; Hattie was crying lustily; and Dennis sat apart, his teeth chattering.

"Pull the curtain, you fool!" shouted his mother, so he climbed on the table and did so just as another blinding flash came. A small china cup on the dresser broke into fragments, and he shot under the table to join his family. Now the heavy rain came beating down and the worst of the storm was over.

"What about some cocoa?" he shouted down his mother's trumpet.

"Yes, those lazy bitches must make cocoa," she said. "We always have cocoa after a thunderstorm.

Come girls, out of the cupboard!"

The maids crept out and lit the smoking paraffin stove and the candles in their brass candlesticks on the mantelpiece, and the occasional flashes were not so visible.

As he watched Norah working, Ebin noticed that she had a great mole shaped like the map of Australia on her chest. She saw he had ginger-beer bottle tops wired onto his pyjamas instead of buttons.

"Poor man," she thought, "we are a lazy lot."

During the days that followed they had little time for laziness. The carpets had to be dragged onto the lawns to dry and the mud washed off the floors and furniture; the house had not had such a cleaning for years. Most of the heavy work fell on Emma and the two maids. Grandmother Willoweed went from one worker to another brandishing a wicker carpet-beater, and if anyone was not working to her satisfaction they received a whack with it. The two children were put on to furniture polishing, which they did in a half-hearted fashion. Dennis knelt on a book, which he read when his grandmother was out of sight. Eunice called to her sister:

"Have you heard that Grumpy Nan who lived in the cottage by the mill was drowned?"

"Yes, poor woman," her sister answered, "but she has been dying this long time. They say she had cancer and suffered something awful, the poor thing! You could hear her groans as you passed the cottage. Yes, it's a merciful release."

Crack! The wicker beater came across her back.

Subdued, the sisters bent over their work. Emma passed them with one arm outstretched to balance the weight of the bucket she carried. She emptied the dirty water it contained down the great brown sink. A smooth white cat had been sitting on the draining board watching intently the water dripping from the pump. It jumped on to her shoulder and rubbed its face against her neck. She stroked it absent-mindedly; but her hands were wet and the cat leapt to the dark stone floor and looked at her with reproachful yellow eyes.

Into the scullery her father tripped. Although he was a large man he always walked on his toes, rather leaning forward with his shoulders hunched.

"He is like a gingerbread man," his daughter thought, "ginger hair, ginger moustache, ginger tweed suit."

He put his breakfast tray on the draining board. He always had breakfast in bed. It was usually taken up to his room by Hattie; the maids seldom went to his room, and his bed was often left unmade for days. When he had deposited the tray, which was decorated with crusts and congealed egg yoke, he put his arms round his daughter, hugged her hard and kissed the back of her neck. She pushed him away impatiently.

"Oh, alright, I was only being affectionate," he said crossly, "Where is your grandmother?"

"Oh, somewhere prowling around. She is in a rage."

"Is she indeed? It's all this cleaning, I suppose; but she can't expect me to help; my hands are my best feature, and they would be ruined. Anyway I loathe housework, and any man who does it is a fool — or any woman for that matter. What's that saying about a whistling hen and a working woman? . . . I don't know," and he stretched his arms and gave a large yawn. "I think I'll go and see Dr. Hatt. There won't be any cleaning women there because I hear his wife is away ill in a nursing home. Change of life, I expect," and he gave a titter and wandered out through the back door.

"Father makes me hate men," thought Emma as she pumped water into the bucket. A slug tumbled out of the pump and she caught it and put it in a dark damp corner under the sink.

"Poor creature," she thought, "if the maids find it, it will be burnt; but, if I put it outside, it will be found by Ives and put in a bucket of salt or fed to the ducks."

CHAPTER II

Ebin Willoweed walked down the village street with his tripping walk. He unsuccessfully tried to get into conversation with several passers-by; but they were hurrying home to their twelve o'clock dinner. The labourers were carrying forks over their shoulders. Each prong had a large potato stuck on it. In theory this was for safety; but actually they achieved about eight potatoes a day by this ruse. Ebin went a little way over the bridge, which was built of stones from the Alcester Monastery by the Normans. The stones had been worn away in several places by generations of butchers sharpening their knives on them.

He stood looking down at the river, which had returned to its banks, but was flowing very fast and full. In some way the river flowing with such purpose and determination depressed Willoweed. He felt humiliated and a failure in everything he undertook; the thought of all those half-completed, mouse-nibbled manuscripts in his room saddened him even more. He bit his lower lip and gave the bridge a kick; then turned away towards Dr. Hatt's house. Dr. Hatt was an old family friend, and regarded by the villagers as a miracle man since he had brought Hattie into the world after her mother's death. She had been named after him.

Willoweed walked up the steep flight of steps that led to the doctor's house and rang the highly polished brass bell with the word 'Visitors' engraved on it. An elderly servant with a twisted back came to the door, and asked him into the cool, flagstoned hall while she hobbled off to find Dr. Hatt. Francis Hatt was a rather melancholy-looking man until he smiled; then his whole face lit up in a delightful way and people talking to him often found themselves saying all manner of wild things to try to bring this smile back to his grave face. This morning he was distressed by his wife's sudden illness and felt he could hardly bear Ebin Willoweed's company. Nevertheless he asked his servant to bring some sherry, and decided to give half an hour to his old, but rather trying friend.

It was over ten years ago that Ebin had returned to his mother's house bringing with him his beautiful young wife and Emma, then a child of seven. The *Daily Courier* which employed him as a gossip writer, had dismissed him because his carelessness had resulted in a libel action which had cost them a considerable amount of money. Jenny Willoweed was expecting a baby at that time, and Dr. Hatt attended her at her very difficult confinement. After Dennis's birth he warned her that it might kill her to have another child. Eighteen months later she died giving birth to Hattie. She died some minutes before the child was born, but Francis Hatt had saved the child's life. In the years that followed Ebin Willoweed had turned to the Doctor for friendship and used his house as a place of refuge from his mother. Francis Hatt had been shocked by the deterioration that had occurred in him; but, although he often found him tiresome, he had devoted a lot of his time to him at first in the hope of providing some stimulus and later from pity.

Ebin Willoweed had hoped to be asked to stay for lunch; but no invitation materialised. He felt discouraged by the doctor's distracted manner and suddenly took his departure, still feeling depressed in spite of the sherry.

When he reached home he had a solitary lunch. The family had already eaten theirs. He caught sight of his mother ascending the stairs, still carrying the wicker carpet-beater and half-heartedly bashing a fly with it. She looked over the banisters and shouted, "You're late, and your hair wants cutting," then continued her climb to her bedroom for her afternoon sleep.

As soon as she was enclosed in her peppermint-smelling room a drowsy peacefulness descended on the house. The maids went up the back stairs to the bedroom they shared, and took off the striped print frocks they wore in the morning. Eunice lay on their bed dressed only in a large white chemise, while Norah washed in a cracked china bowl. She held up her hair with one hand, and with the other worked away with a soapy flannel. The large mole on her chest showed above her camisole. When she had finished her toilet she rinsed the bowl and wiped it carefully with a cloth; but Eunice, when it was her turn to wash, left the basin filled with dark, scummy water. As they dressed in their black afternoon frocks they quarrelled over this. Then Norah lent her sister her silver brooch with Amelia, their dead mother's name engraved on it, and they were happy again and sat in the window with their arms around each other, looking down on the village street.

In the garden old Ives was tying up the flowers that had been damaged by the flood. While he worked he talked to his ducks, who were waddling about hopefully, as it was almost time for the red bucket to be filled with sharps and potato-peelings. Emma dawdled up to him and said:

"Don't you think, Ives, we should send a wreath to Grumpy Nan's funeral? It's tomorrow, and people seem to be making a great fuss about it."

"Of course they are making a fuss, her being drowned and all. It's a long time since we had a drowning by flood; that's an important event in this village. And don't you worry about the wreath neither. I was just telling my ducks as you came along about the pretty wreath I'm going to make this evening. White peonies it will be made of, Miss, and little green grapes. There won't be another to touch it, will there, my dears?" and he turned to the ducks who agreed with him in chorus.

"Thank you, Ives," she said, "no one makes wreaths like you;" and she left him still talking to his white birds.

"If ever I die," she thought, "I'd like a wreath of water lilies, only they'd go brown so soon."

She came to a swing that hung from a pine tree near the river. Once when she had been swinging on it she had disturbed a bumble-bee from above, and it came buzzing out from the pines and was as large as a lemon; but when she told people about this they wouldn't believe her and said it must have been a buzzing bird. She sat in the swing now in the hope of seeing this strange insect again. She swung for a few minutes; but no lemon-sized bee appeared. So she sat quite still dreamily gazing at the shining river between the pine trees.

She had pinned her hair in a large knot at the nape of her neck, and she felt very conscious of her altered appearance.

"But no one will notice," she thought.

She looked down at her little feet in the clumsy shoes made by the village cobbler, and she felt like crying. Even Eunice wore pointed black shoes with high heels on her day out. Twice a year the cobbler, who was also the village bookmaker, came to the house by the river and measured the feet of anyone who needed new shoes; and a week or two later he came again with some clumsy pieces of leather heavily nailed together. It was the same when Emma or Hattie needed new clothes. Lolly Bennet would be summoned from the little house that you had to go down steps to reach the front door. She was the village old maid, and almost a dwarf. It was with great difficulty that she managed the great bales of cloth provided by Grandmother Willoweed, who stood over the poor little thing as she crawled about the floor with her mouth full of pins trying to cut dresses with the aid of paper patterns.

"You will waste the material if you cut it like that, you little freak. Good God! Don't you know how to make a gusset? If you let your hands shake like that you will cut the material to ribbons," and so it went on. The results of Lolly Bennet's labours were lumpy and bunchy, and dipped at the back and cut across the shoulders. Grandmother Willoweed had not added to her own wardrobe for twenty-five years and she still wore a form of bustle.

As Emma sat swinging gently she felt overcome with a longing for beautiful clothes and an admirer, or several admirers; overcome with a longing to travel, perhaps even in a private yacht. She imagined a white one gliding through impossibly blue water, and saw herself on deck wearing an evening gown with a train. And then there was the tango. How beautiful it would be to tango to exotic music, and perhaps go to something called a tango tea! Her thoughts were disturbed by the sound of shrill chirping and she remembered she had not fed the small chickens that had been bought to replace the ones that had been drowned . . .

She wandered towards the kitchen, and there was Norah sitting in the Windsor armchair, staring into space with unseeing eyes. On her lap was her best black straw hat, which she was absentmindedly stabbing with a hatpin.

Norah had spent the afternoon in the damp cottage where Fig the gardener lived with his mother. The village people rightly called Mrs. Fig a dirty little body. Her cottage was so filthy it was almost uninhabitable; but recently Norah had devoted her free afternoons to bringing some kind of order to the place. This afternoon, as she scrubbed floors and beat mats, Mrs. Fig had sat huddled over the fire and talked in her soft dreamy voice. Occasionally a stray tear slipped from her protruding, misty blue eyes. Her only garment was a greasy old mackintosh all gathered together with pins; it smelt sour. She was the village layer-out. When Fig returned for his tea, instead of the soggy bread that smelt of paraffin and the jar of fish paste with green mould on top which were usually arranged on a newspaper, there was a neatly laid table with a newly-baked cake. All around there was a strong smell of soap and floor polish.

Fig drew down his long upper lip and scowled. Much as he disliked his mother's filthy ways, he resented Norah's interference even more. For some time he had suspected she was cleaning his mother's cottage; now he knew. He sat down at the table with barely a nod to Norah and morosely ate her cake. She tried to make conversation and talked about the coming Coronation; but he only answered in monosyllables and the meal ended in complete silence.

When he had finished eating, he pushed his chair back from the table and stood biting his nails for a moment. Then he went into the garden and started thinning carrots. Norah watched him from the window. She thought his long, sallow face the most handsome she had ever seen. "He's like a Puritan," she thought. Half-heartedly she listened to his mother's gently complaining voice; then turned from the window and put on her hat and picked up her white cotton gloves.

When she had said goodbye to Mrs. Fig she left the cottage. She had to pass Fig as she walked down the narrow cinder path. When she drew near him, she stopped and held up one of the net curtains that covered the currant bushes.

"How well the currants are coming on, Mr. Fig," she called gaily; but he only grunted and bent over the carrots. She turned away and sadly opened the gate. As she did so, she noticed two snails crawling over the grey-green wood. She suddenly took them off and hurled them across the road. Their shells cracked on the stones, and she looked over her shoulder at Fig; but he was still bent over the carrots.

As Norah sat on that Windsor chair sticking pins in her best hat, her mind went over the events of the afternoon, and she wondered why Fig so persistently ignored her. Perhaps if she was as pretty as Eunice things would be different. Maybe she would take some of her savings from the post office and buy a new frock; or she could buy one through her club and pay so much a week. She had just finished paying for the grey corsets she was wearing; so she could afford to buy a dress. She imagined herself walking through the meadows on Fig's arm. They would pass other couples

and everyone would know they were "walking out";
their shoes would be new and shiny and make squeaks
as they walked; perhaps they would sit on the river
bank when it became dusk . . . . Norah's sadness departed, and she glanced round the room as if she had
only just discovered herself there. When she saw
Emma looking at her, she smiled and helped her chop
up hard boiled eggs for the chickens. Afterwards they
went down the garden together to pick peas for
supper, and to dream their dreams in the summer
dusk.

CHAPTER III

IT was Grandmother Willoweed's birthday. She was
seventy one. Directly breakfast was finished, and
while she was sitting behind the silver teapot still
gently chewing, Old Ives came in with a basket of
duck eggs and some Hog's Pudding as a birthday offering. They always exchanged birthday gifts, and each
was determined to outlive the other. Ives was a year
older than Grandmother Willoweed, but considered he
had the better chance of survival: He thought she
would die from overeating. The grandmother thanked
him for his presents and said, "Ah, Ives, I'm afraid,
when it's your birthday, I shall be bringing flowers for
your grave."

The old man replied, "Do you think so, Ma'am?
Well, I know you will have stuffed yourself until you
be choked by the time your next birthday comes
round."

"Well, we shall see," Grandmother Willoweed said
quite imperturbably. "I expect I shall last out the day
and enjoy my meals as well; so perhaps you will be so
good as to cut plenty of roses and bring them to the

22

house some time this morning. I'm having my annual whist drive this afternoon."

Every year on her birthday she gave a whist drive. No one enjoyed it very much. The tenant farmers' wives (she owned three farms) used to attend, and Dr. Hatt and his wife, and the sleepy clergyman and his mother. Grandmother Willoweed always declared the clergyman took opium, perhaps because he rather resembled a Chinaman. His mother was a little frightened bird of a woman, who held her twisted, claw-like hands clasped near her face as if she was praying. This made it rather difficult for her to play cards and they would fall round her like the petals from a dying flower. The three old maids from Roary Court would come on their tricycles. Their pet billy goat would trot behind them as they rode down the village street, and they would tether him where he could be seen from the drawing room window. He had a mania for eating ivy, and, when he had finished all the ivy within his reach at Roary Court, the old ladies had put a step ladder at his disposal. It looked rather unusual to see this great black and white goat perched on a ladder, gorging away on the ivy that was wrapped all round their house.

The village bachelor, drink-sodden Lumber Splinterbones, usually ambled along to Grandmother Willoweed's birthday party. He was a grey-haired giant of a man, who stank of beer, but was gentle and kind. He never became really drunk, nor was he ever entirely sober. He was so heavy he had broken several of the Willoweed chairs, and a hefty Irish Chippendale chair with arms was now reserved for him. The old maids from Roary Court thought he needed mothering and quarrelled over him quite a lot. Lame Lawyer Williams would drive over with his wife and anaemic daughter. He looked after the Willoweed money and, whenever he came to the house, Ebin Willoweed would buttonhole him in a corner and try to discover how much money his mother actually had and how she had disposed of it in her will. No doubt he would do so today with his usual lack of success. Ebin had inherited one hundred a year from his wife after her death. It wasn't very much; but it meant he was not entirely dependent on his mother. It was years since he had earned anything from writing. When Emma came of age the hundred a year passed to her. This worried Ebin considerably. Unless his mother died before then, he would be completely penniless. Sometimes in the night he thought about the future quite a lot.

When it became afternoon and the guests began to arrive, Emma stood beside her grandmother to receive them. Grandmother Willoweed wore a magenta gown trimmed with black lace, and on her head three purple plumes attached to a piece of dusty velvet. The magenta gown was split in several places; but she considered it was the general effect that mattered. Emma wore a green tussore dress she had made herself. It had a tightly fitting bodice and a long gathered skirt. It was the first time she had worn it and she thought it a great success. Perhaps it wasn't quite the success she thought; but the green suited her vivid colouring—although, when she and her grandmother stood side by side receiving their guests, the magenta and green did look rather strident against the browns and blacks of the visitors. Lumber Splinterbones was quite overcome by Emma's appearance, and made several clumsy grabs at her before he could be persuaded to sit at a card table.

When all the guests were seated and had begun playing, Emma slipped away. She remembered whist drives when her grandmother had failed to win the first prize and there had been piercing screams and roars of anger. This time the first prize consisted of several pots of pâte-de-foie-gras, and she knew her grandmother was looking forward to eating them at night in bed. The tenant farmers' wives were well trained; but some of the guests were not to be depended on. The second prize was quite harmless—just a silver toast-rack.

Emma went down the long stone passage to the kitchen, and collected a picnic-basket Norah had prepared for her. There was a great tumult in the kitchen. Eunice was giving a final polish to the silver tea-service, and all around there were cakes and sandwiches. Old Ives was looking very self-conscious dressed up as a waiter, and Norah was almost in tears because the range had gone out and there was no hot water. Emma took the basket unobserved and hurried down to the river, where Hattie and Dennis were waiting in the rowing boat. She felt guilty she had not offered to help in the kitchen; but she was glad to have escaped. She and Hattie each took an oar. Dennis had a whole fleet of boats tied to various pieces of string. Sometimes one or the other of them would capsize and the small boy dashed from one side of the boat to the other putting them to rights.

When the girls tired of rowing they tied the boat up under a willow tree. It seemed as if they were in a green tent. They sat there for a little time; but the bottom of the boat smelt of fish, so they climbed out and lay on the river bank in the sun. The river breeze rustled the rushes and made a whispering sound. After a time Emma opened the picnic basket and they ate honey sandwiches with ants on them and drank the queer tea that always comes from a thermos. When there was no more picnic fare left they lay in the sun again in a straight line, and became very warm and watched dragon-flies. Some were light blue, small and elegant; others were a shining green; and there were enormous stripey ones that took large bites out of the water-lily leaves.

As Dennis lay in the sun, he thought how pleasant it was having a picnic with Emma in charge. He remembered other afternoons when his father had forced him to bathe from the boat, and, when he had clutched at the sides with his terrified hands, his father had bashed his fingers with a paddle and laughed and yelled at his struggles in the water. When at last he was allowed to climb back, his teeth used to chatter. That seemed to make his father laugh even more. He used to lie at the bottom of the boat while his father laughed and Emma dried him, grumbling at their father as she rubbed with a towel. So far this year there had not been any of those dreadful bathes. For sometimes the floods made the river unsuitable for boating and now Willoweed hardly noticed the children. It was weeks since they had had their morning lessons. They guessed this would go on until their grandmother suddenly realized what was happening. Then there would be a great tornado, in which their father would become almost crushed to a pulp, and the lessons would start again with new vigour, until Grandmother Willoweed lost interest in them and they would gradually peter out again. Dennis often wondered why his father, who seemed to set such store by bravery, was always so cowed by his mother. He thought perhaps it was chivalry.

The sun was very warm and there was the sound of music gradually coming nearer. A boat passed with a gramophone with a large green horn. A man in a striped blazer was punting, and a woman with golden hair sat under a red parasol. She changed a record on the gramophone and a grunting, wailing organ filled the air. 'How I hate organs' thought Emma, 'I'm sure people who like organs eat cheese cakes and call their drawing rooms lounges.' She lay on her back imagining the golden haired woman sitting in her lounge, eating eternal cheese cakes and listening to a fruity organ. She would have several little girls she called "the kiddies." They would have crimped hair with large pink bows on the top, and wear patent-leather shoes and shiny satin bridesmaids' frocks on summer Sundays. Then she forgot about the family of cheese-cake-and-organ-lovers because the children seemed to have vanished. She sat up and saw they were in the field behind, throwing stones into cow pats; so she turned her back on them and sat watching the river.

She called to the children and they left off their disgusting game and returned. Hattie was carrying a rusty tin filled with newts they had caught with their hands in a nearby pond. They insisted on putting them in the boat to take home. Then it was discovered that all the strings of Dennis's boats had become entangled and had to be sorted out before the boats would float properly. Emma rather welcomed these delays. She wanted to be certain the whist drive had really ended before she returned. She rowed home with leisurely strokes. There was no sound of screams coming from the house; so she gathered the party had been a success from her grandmother's point of view.

The guests had all departed, and the maids were folding up the card tables in the drawing room. Then she heard her grandmother calling, "Emma, Emma," in her nasal voice.

"Please God, don't let her be in one of her rages," prayed Emma, as she hurried to the dining room, where her grandmother's excited voice seemed to be coming from. Grandmother Willoweed was pouring herself a glass of port. Both the ends of her tongue were protruding—rather a bad sign. When she saw Emma standing there looking so apprehensive, she put her glass down on the sideboard and said, "Doctor Hatt was called away in the middle of my whist drive. His wife was worse—her nose was bleeding." She filled her glass from the decanter and gave Emma a strange glance.

"Well, peoples' noses are always bleeding. You are supposed to put a large key down their back."

Emma was rather perplexed at her grandmother making such a commotion about such an ordinary happening. Perhaps she was annoyed about the numbers of the whist drive being upset.

Grandmother Willoweed took a sip of port, and looked with her lizardlike eyes over her glass.

"Well, my dear, a key wouldn't have been much use in this case; this was a peculiar kind of nosebleed. It went on and on until the bed became filled with blood—at least that is what I heard—it went on and on and the mattress was soaked and the floor became crimson; it went on and on until Mrs. Hatt died."

She took another sip of port.

"Yes, Mrs. Hatt is dead now."

She looked hopefully at Emma to see if she was sufficiently shocked and surprised.

Emma remembered Mrs. Hatt's comfortable figure and the brown plaits twisted round her head. She recalled helping her make marmalade last spring. Would all that marmalade be wasted now? People couldn't eat dead people's marmalade, surely—and the Christmas puddings hanging up in her kitchen? Doctor Hatt couldn't very well have a merry Christmas eating his dead wife's pudding while she was lying so cold in the churchyard. Emma saw her grandmother watching her, her trumpet already at her ear, waiting for the words of surprise and sorrow; so she did her best. But her grandmother looked disappointed.

"You are a selfish girl, Emma, just like your mother. Other people's sorrows mean nothing to you. I remember when the tom cat ate the salmon Cousin Tweed sent me from Scotland, your mother actually laughed—and another time when I burnt my lip on a hot chestnut . . ."

But Emma had gone, so she finished her port and wandered off in the hope of finding someone who had not heard about Mrs. Hatt's death.

She eventually made for the potting shed, where she found old Ives stewing a pigeon on his slow, but sure, combustion stove. Her audience was rather limited because for many years she had not left her own house and garden. She had an objection to walking or passing over ground that did not belong to her. For that reason she never visited the farms she owned. She would have had to pass through the village to reach them. Most of the village children had never seen her and she had become a terrifying figure in their minds. They thought she could hear everything they said with her ear trumpet, and that instead of a tongue she had two curling snakes in her ugly mouth. When the children grew up and some of them became maids in Willowed House they were almost disappointed to discover she wasn't so strange as they expected; but they told their friends how she had three freak moles all stuffed in her bedroom on a bamboo table, and that she had catgut laces in her corsets, and how they would often hear her whistling to herself in bed in the mornings when they took in her early morning tea—also that she used to eat black biscuits out of tins. They told these things in hushed whispers and they sounded sinister and dreadful. Then there were always stories to tell of the quantities of food she devoured and her raging tempers, and there were often bruises to be displayed.

CHAPTER IV

O LD IVES sat in the potting shed weaving a wreath of roses and thyme for Mrs. Hatt's grave—full bloom roses because she was a full blown woman, although she had never had a child. Ives liked to choose suitable flowers for his wreathes. He often planned the one he would make for Grandmother Willoweed: — thistles and hogswart and grey-green holly — sometimes he would grant her one yellow dandelion. Ebin was to have one of bindweed and tobacco plants. Quite often people would die when the flowers already chosen for them were not in season. Then he made a temporary wreath for them, and months later they received the real one. At this moment he could see the old woman pacing to and fro on the top path, and he laughed to himself because he knew what was worrying her.

Grandmother Willoweed paced to and fro with her determined tread. Impatiently she kicked a tortoise that happened to impede her. She gnawed her horny thumb nail as she concentrated on the problem of attending the funeral without passing over ground

that did not belong to her. Then her glance fell on the
river shining between the fir trees, and suddenly the
problem was solved. She would travel to the Church
by boat. It would mean that the weir by the bridge
would have to be opened for the occasion; but that
was nothing. She strode towards the potting shed to
give Ives his funeral orders. The old punt could be
draped in black, and Ebin and Ives would attend her.
She could see herself sailing in state under the bridge,
the great black plumes on her hat gently swaying.

While the two old people discussed tomorrow's
funeral, Hattie and Dennis played with the peacock on
the round lawn in front of the house. They fed it with
breadcrumbs that had become hard and dry in
Dennis's pocket. The boy gave a startled cry as the
great bird pecked his hand.

"No, hold your hand flat like this, and he won't
peck," said Hattie; but he threw the crumbs on the
grass where they were eagerly pounced on by waiting sparrows. The peacock spread his tail in anger and
walked backwards, his feathers vibrating with
emotion; but his furious beauty made no impression
on the sparrows. The children watched for a moment,
then wandered down to the river, where they were
making a harbour in the roots of an old willow tree.
Across the river they could see Eunice walking in the
large flat meadow among the cows. The meadow had
been divided so that half of it could be used for hay,
and today young Joe Lott had started to cut the outer
edge. The children watched and imagined they could
already smell the hay. When Joe came near Eunice,

she crossed to the fence, and he stopped the horse and they talked and laughed together. Then he mockingly drank Eunice's health from a brown bottle. The children knew the bottle only contained cold, bitter tea, because they had often drunk from the haymakers' bottles and found them disappointing. Ives came down to the river carrying a large bundle of rusty black material, which he dumped on the landing stage; and cursing and grumbling he started to bale out the old punt. The children heard his angry mutterings and crept away to the strawberry beds.

It was one of those early summer afternoons when there is a constant hum of insects. Down the village street pranced the baker's wife. About her florid face she wore a Dolly Varden bonnet, and the bodice of her dress was transparent and the pink ribbons of her camisole could be clearly seen. The women of the village said her face was rough with kisses. Sometimes in the "Masons' Arms" the men would discuss how far they had walked to see their wives when they were courting them. They would turn to the baker and remark that it was unlikely that he had had to walk far.

Ebin watched the Baker's wife's progress through the village from his attic window. Then he combed his hair and moustache in front of his discoloured mirror, filled his tobacco pouch and started to leave the room. He seemed to change his mind for a moment, and stood frowning; but eventually he hurried out and ran lightly down the stairs. As he crossed the hall he heard his mother's voice. He hesitated; then crept from the house. His mother called again and came clumping into the hall. Seeing it empty she went into the boot-room, which had a good view of the street. Peering through the stained-glass window she saw her son all crimson following a yellow baker's wife. Then they changed colour and both became green and disappeared from sight.

While his wife planned to spend the afternoon in pleasure on the river bank, Emblyn the baker worked in the heat of his bakery icing a wedding cake for the postman's daughter. He was a small grey-faced man. He had recently developed stomach ulcers which caused him considerable pain; but in spite of the pain and distress he suffered, his bread was still the best in Warwickshire. The paper it was wrapped in was stamped with his name, "Horace Emblyn" and reproductions of his medals. Disappointed in his marriage, he devoted his life to the bakery; and his loaves were so delicious and crusty, and his sponge cakes such a miracle of lightness, and his fruit cakes so rich and damp, that people for miles round begged for them. But he would only serve the inhabitants of the village, and they kept him working all the day and half the night. His only assistant was a young boy—on whom the baker suspected, his wife was already casting glances. As he worked an intricate design of flowers and doves in snowy icing on the bridal cake, his thoughts wandered and he planned to make a few loaves of rye bread as an experiment. He forgot his wife and the pinching pain inside him and happiness came instead.

Happiness also came to Norah on that summer

afternoon. She was returning from Bennet's fruit
farm, where she had been ordering quantities of
strawberries to be used for the Willoweeds' jam. The
road she walked was white with dust, but the deep
verges on either side were still brilliant green all
decorated with cow parsley like spangles and with tall
buttercups. As she crossed over the little bridge that
divided Worcestershire from Warwickshire, she heard
carriage wheels and, turning round, she saw Fig driving Doctor Hatt's gig and the dust flying round him
like a shroud. She desperately hoped he would not
pass without speaking, and, when he stopped and
offered her a lift, she was so surprised that she climbed
in beside him without uttering a word. Fig muttered
something about meeting Doctor Hatt's London rela-
tions at Honeywell Station and how they had not
been on the train and his journey had been wasted.
'Not wasted,' thought Norah, as she drove through the
village like a queen. They reached the gates of Willoweed House without speaking; but, when Norah
looked up to thank him, she looked so pretty with her
usually pale, plain face all lit up that Fig found himself asking her to visit his mother again.

"You do her so much good," he said, and then drove
away dismayed at his own folly and weakness.

Norah opened the great dark gates in a dream of
happiness. When she got back to the house, she hardly
noticed the fact that her sister was not there; nor did
she notice when Eunice returned later, that her dress
was strangely crumpled and buttons were missing
from her bodice.

CHAPTER V

EARLY in the morning the sun came streaming into Emma's room. The reflected light from the river made golden patterns on the wall. She got up, dressed quickly, stole out of the sleeping house, and ran down to the water. Moored to the landing-stage was the old punt in rusty black, decorated here and there by dreaming moths. When she knelt down to untie the canoe, the boards of the landing-stage were already so hot from the sun she could feel the heat through her dress. She stepped into the light little boat and glided away on the still water. She felt completely happy. She was alone except for a swan and its family of cygnets. The swan gently passed. There were fields on either side of the river. Some were freshly green where the hay had already been cut, and one was all sparkling blue with early cabbages. In a small bay a group of cows stood knee-deep in the water and gracefully turned their heads to watch her as she passed. She came to a little wrecked pleasure-steamer, which had become embedded in the mud several summers ago and which no one had bothered to remove. It had been a vulgar, tubby little boat when it used to steam through the water with its handful of holiday-makers, giving shrill whistles at every bend and causing a wash that disturbed the fishermen as they sat peacefully on the banks; but, now it lay sideways in the mud with its gaudy paint all bleached, it was almost beautiful.

The morning stillness was broken by a young sheep dog's excited barking, then by the voices of some farm-hands driving a cart into a field. Disturbed from her quiet happiness, Emma realized that she was hungry and her dress wet from the water that ran down the double paddle. As she turned the boat homewards, suddenly she noticed that the muddy banks of the river had grown much deeper and that the water seemed to be receding. She remembered that during haymaking season the river was sometimes lowered so that carts could cross at the fords.

When she reached the landing-stage she saw Dennis lying on his stomach, looking into the water. She called him; but he did not answer, and she knew he was hurt because she had not taken him with her.

"Dennis," she called again, "do you know they are letting out the water?"

The little boy jumped up and examined his harbour in the willow-tree's roots.

"Yes, look! It's gone down quite six inches already!"

Happy again, he rushed away to tell Hattie. The children loved to dig in the exposed mud for treasure; and although they did this at least twice a summer there were always new embedded treasures — small pieces of coloured glass and china, keys, farthings, rusty corkscrews, long-lost lead soldiers, and once, a shilling and a large china dog.

Emma entered the house through the kitchen, and a great smell of frying bacon met her.   Norah was preparing a tray for her grandmother.

"Three duck eggs and all this bacon, Miss Emma," she muttered crossly.

"The master's coming down this morning, so perhaps you'd better call him; we can't have meals hanging about all day!"

So Emma went to call her father; but, to her surprise, met him coming down his attic stairs all dressed in black and smelling of camphor.

"Breakfast ready?" he asked haughtily as he passed.

Astounded, Emma went to her room to do her hair, which was pouring down her back. She tried puffing it out at the sides, with a very low bun at the back, and from a drawer concealed by a nightgown she produced a silver mirror. She admired her changed appearance for a few moments; then carefully hid the mirror, which she had taken from her mother's room on one of the few occasions her grandmother had left it unlocked.

As she went down to the dining room she could hear her father complaining bitterly because breakfast was not on the table. When at last it was ready, Norah banged the gong so ferociously that Grandmother Willoweed hurled a brass candlestick down the stairs. All through the meal Hattie and Dennis gazed at their father. Dennis dared to say "I say, you do look posh,

Father!'' and his father glanced at him coldly and
said, "I have not worn these clothes since your dear
Mother died."

The almost silent meal was disturbed by a loud
knock at the door, and Ives appeared beaming all over
his face. "I want to speak to the old Mistress," he
almost shouted. "She can't go to the funeral up that
little old river because it won't be there, not to notice,
it won't."

"What nonsense is this?" Grandmother Willoweed
asked.

She had entered the room behind Ives, and no one
had noticed her, which was strange considering the
fantastic figure she made. She looked like a dreadful
old black bird, enormous and horrifying, all weighed
down by jet and black plumes and smelling, not of
camphor, but chlorodyne.

There was an uproar for a few minutes while the
two old people shouted at each other. Then, with Ebin
walking morosely behind, they went down to inspect
the river, and the children sat at the breakfast table
laughing and crying at the same time.

At eleven thirty the sinister black group were still
arguing by the river, while the sun beat down on their
heads. Eventually it was decided by Grandmother
Willoweed that the boat could be dragged through the
mud to the water.

"But who will wade through all that mud?" wailed
her son.

"You, of course, my dear, with a little help from
Ives."

"Mother, my clothes!" he shouted.

"You are dressed like a fool already, so what does it matter?" the old woman snapped, swinging her ear trumpet around in a threatening manner.

Ives went off to the potting shed and returned with two enormous pairs of waders that were sometimes use for fishing by the weir. Dejectedly the men crawled into them.

"Hurry, hurry!" their persecutor shouted, and her tongue protruded through her lips.

Without a word the men stepped into the mud and dragged and pushed the heavy old boat towards the water. They struggled in the mud and heaved and pushed, and in the end they did manage to get the boat into quite deep water. Ives remained holding it while Ebin returned for his mother. She almost leapt at him and twined her great legs round his body, and he reeled under her weight. Staggering and gasping, he managed to reach the funeral barge and push his awful mother into it. Relieved of her weight, he lent, doubled up, over the boat. Channels of sweat were pouring down his swollen, almost crimson face. Old Ives helped him gently into the boat; they were fellow sufferers.

When Ebin had sufficiently recovered, the men used punt poles and found the boat moved quite easily. Grandmother Willoweed sat in her draped arm-chair, a proud but rather muddy figure. She looked straight ahead, which was just as well or she would have seen Eunice's laughing face looking at her between the trees and Hattie convulsed with laughter sitting on the hen-pen roof. Ives's ducks watched the boat's progress from the island where they were preening themselves in the sun, and when the boat drew near most of them flew into the water with loud quacks of welcome.

"Send those foolish birds away!" complained the old woman; but Ives took no notice and they followed hopefully behind.

Quite a crowd had collected on the bridge. Many of them had never seen Grandmother Willoweed, and this was their chance. There were cries of "Here she is! There she is! Look at the old girl! Oh, my, ain't she like a witch? Just look at Mr. Ives all dressed like a toff! Do you think they will stick in the mud?"

Ebin was overcome with shame and confusion; but his mother, who was unable to hear their remarks, thought the village was paying her homage, and bowed gravely.

The weir was near the bridge, so the crowd was entertained with the spectacle of the two men wading into the water and mud and struggling to open it and drag the boat through. The churchyard sloped down to the river. Ebin had to carry his mother across the mud while Ives waded behind bearing his sadly wilted wreath. The ducks had fortunately been eluded. A number of people hurried to the bank and jeered and tittered as Ebin staggered under the old woman's weight. Within a few weeks funerals were to become a common occurrence in that village; but at this time they were rather scarce and looked forward to eagerly.

The mourners assembled in the little Norman

church for a short service, and then shambled out. Slowly and with bowed heads they walked to the newly made grave, on one side of which were heaped great clods of earth. Doctor Hatt stood alone like a man in a dream. He seemed absent from his wife's funeral. The mid-day sun burned down on the black group of people. They looked like bloated, sleepy flies at the end of the season. They were imprisoned by tombstones tumbling in all directions, some beautiful and others so rotted away that large holes had appeared in the stone, framing the green grass of the churchyard.

As soon as the funeral was over, and before the mourners had hardly left, the uninvited surged into the churchyard to watch the gravedigger fill the grave with the clods of clay so recently removed and to examine the dying wreaths. They were accompanied by many dogs.

CHAPTER VI

Roars of laughter came from the Willoweed coach-house, and rain beat down like bullets on the corrugated iron roof of the Dutch barn. In the coach-house it was almost dark, but the little light that filtered down from the apple-room above revealed Ebin Willoweed embracing the baker's wife in the musty old carriage. Her corsets were draped over the window frame, and other garments were scattered carelessly around. They drank sour stout and laughed and made love, and above them mice gnawed the rotten apples.

In his lonely bakery the baker was experimenting again with his rye bread. He hoped that within a few days he would be able to give a small rye loaf to every customer, and the thought of their surprise and pleasure eased his own unhappiness. So he spent that wet summer afternoon baking his rye bread.

Hattie and Dennis waited for their father in his room. He had left them with Macaulay's "History of England" early in the afternoon; but, as he did not return, they tore out its pages one by one and made

44

them into paper hats and boats. In her room below their grandmother lay on her bed nibbling her charcoal biscuits. She could hear the children above, and thought she could distinguish their father's voice mingled with theirs; and she congratulated herself on having insisted on their lessons being resumed. There had been quite a scene over this; but eventually Ebin had agreed to "coach" his children for several hours a day. He always referred to his spasmodic efforts at teaching his children as "coaching" — it sounded so much better.

His mother lay on her bed remembering the two figures she had seen changing colours in the stained glass of the boot-room window, and thought what a good thing it was she had put a stop to that nonsense. But she was bored. She had had her way; her son was teaching his children; the maids were doing their work; Ives had even agreed to dig over the long-neglected north border, which had become completely choked with ground-elder. She had not really cared if the bed was filled with thistles or ground elder; but she knew Ives dreaded taking a spade to the heavy damp clay of that north bed.

For the last few days Ives's bent old figure could be seen digging away quite happily; and, although she had spent some time standing over him like a slave-driver with a trumpet instead of a whip, no complaints had passed the old man's lips. She did not know that he had recently discovered a small box that had once been decorated with shells buried in that bed. The box had rotted almost away; but the two golden sovereigns and the florins it contained were as bright as ever. So the old man happily dug away in the hope of finding more treasure. He guessed the little box had been hidden by Jenny Willoweed. Perhaps it was a small hoard to help her escape one day. She had escaped without the help of those useful coins. But Ives was worried by his conscience. He very much wanted to keep the contents of the little box; but that afternoon, as he sat in his potting shed waiting for the rain to cease, he decided he would give Emma one gold sovereign and Hattie and Dennis a florin each. He need not say where the money came from.

This problem settled, Ives went out into the rain to fill his old red bucket with sharps from a large bin in the stable. As he crossed over the yard, he heard voices coming from the coach-house. He opened the door a chink; but, when he recognised Ebin Willoweed's voice, he hastily closed it and trotted off to the kitchen to collect the boiled potato skins which were eaten with such relish by his ducks.

Emma had been left in the dining-room by her grandmother surrounded by a mountain of white sheets, which all had large holes and tears. She had mended several with the aid of a small and ancient sewing machine; but, to her horror, the patches were coming off already because the machine was only capable of a rather charming chain stitch and she had forgotten to secure the ends of the thread. She welcomed Eunice with the tea tray, and the two girls talked as they cleared the sheets from the table. Eunice was full of the news that Doctor Hatt was probably going to buy a motor car — "a beautiful yellow one, Miss, called a Sunbeam, and Mr. Fig will have to learn to drive it. Oh, Miss Emma, Norah can hardly wait to see him at the wheel!" cried the excited girl.

Grandmother Willoweed's face, like a swollen wasp, appeared round the door. "What's all this talk. girls?" and she held her trumpet eagerly to her ear. So Eunice told her about the beautiful yellow car, though this time without quite so much enthusiasm. The old woman listened eagerly, but seemed disappointed.

"Oh, is that all?" she remarked bitterly, "When you are as old as I am you will realize that men always behave like fools as soon as their wives die." She suddenly turned to Eunice, "Get out of my way, girl! I want my tea!"

The children came rushing downstairs, for they had heard the sound of clattering tea cups from their father's attic.

"What have you been learning, children?" the grandmother asked.

"Oh, we have been learning Macaulay's 'History of England'," shouted Hattie, and both children started to laugh. The grandmother eyed them with suspicion and demanded to be told the whereabouts of their father.

"He has just gone out in the rain to buy some tobacco. Poor father, he will get very wet," said Hattie, gazing at the old woman with big sad eyes. At that moment Ebin's footsteps passed the door and they heard him creep upstairs. Grandmother Willoweed meditated over a large slice of dark plum cake.

Three days later everyone in the village received a a small rye loaf with their daily bread.

CHAPTER VII

I N SPITE of the rather sinister appearance of the dark little rye loaves the villagers were delighted with them and enjoyed their bitter flavour. Orders for rye bread increased every day, and Emblyn worked even longer hours than usual. He sent his young assistant out with the deliveries and engaged an old and most hideous man called Toby to help in the bakery.

This old man had had his face injured by quick lime in his youth. His eyes were red and his face scarred, but he was an excellent worker and spotlessly clean. He had worked for many years in the kitchen of a large hotel, where he was hidden from the eyes of the guests, but he had suddenly conceived a longing to return to his native village. His memory had painted a picture that was all golden and it seemed to him that people had looked kindly on his disfigured face. In the city, whenever he left his deep, dark kitchen, people stared at him in horror and boys shouted "Been using yer head as a poker old man?" and other cruel remarks. So he returned to the village with his life savings and bought a small cottage in the field across the river. At first he was bitterly disillusioned. He saw the same look of horror on people's faces as he had seen in the city; for the young people had never known him and the old ones had forgotten him. In time, however, everybody came to take his appearance for granted. He joined in all the village activities, and made quite a local reputation from the enormous dahlias he grew amongst the cabbages in his little garden. He did not need the money he earned in the bakery but he liked the work and was grateful to the little baker, who had been the first man to show him friendship on his return. He guessed that one of the reasons that the baker had chosen him as an assistant was that there was little risk of his attracting his wife; but he was glad enough of this as he was terrified of women.

When old Toby had been working at the bakery for about ten days, Eunice came in to order a large seed cake for the Willoweeds. It was a sultry afternoon, and the smell of baking and then the sight of poor old Toby's red eyes and scarred face suddenly sickened her. She felt her upper lip become damp and a great noise of rushing, like a thousand pigeons' wings, came in her ears. She sat on a sack of flour and buried her face in her hands, and Toby hurried to fetch her water, his poor face all puckered up with worry. Eunice felt better when she had drank a little; and was just managing to get to her feet when a boy came rushing into the bakery and shouted, "Hi! The miller has gone mad and drowned himself. They are just fishing his body out of the river now!" Before they could question him he was gone. The baker came running out of the bakehouse calling, "What was that? What has happened?" and his wife who had been drinking suddenly appeared and said, "What's th'matter?" and stood there swaying.

Eunice left without ordering the seed cake, she felt strangely sick and longed to lie down in the cool and quiet of her bedroom. But, when she reached the Willoweed house, all was confusion. Grandmother Willoweed had heard the news and wanted Emma to row her down the river to see the miller's body dragged out of the water. She shouted at her and shook her; but poor Eunice only cried, "No! No!" in a pitiful voice. The noise reached Ebin's attic, and he crept down the stairs, holding the banister so that he could retreat quickly before he became involved in anything unpleasant. When he heard what all the commotion was about, he was not at all averse to seeing the drowned miller himself, and offered to take his mother. The words were hardly out of his mouth before the old woman seized his arm and almost dragged him down to the water.

"Hurry, hurry, or we will be too late," she cried as she took a flying leap into the boat, which shivered under the sudden weight.

In spite of the heat Ebin rowed swiftly while his mother urged him on, and they soon came to a small group of empty boats. On the bank of the river there were about a dozen people gazing at Doctor Hatt, assisted by the miller's son, giving the drowned miller artificial respiration — with no results. The miller very dead and his eyes were horribly wide open.

"I'm sorry; but it's no use," said the doctor, "he has been dead about an hour. We must get him back to the mill."

They decided to lay the corpse on a blanket in the bottom of a boat, which the son could tow to the mill. Doctor Hatt shut the dreadful open eyes; but they were were soon open again with their glassy stare. One of the villagers stepped forward and placed pennies on the eyes to weigh the lids down; but, when they carried him to the boat, the pennies fell out and there were the dreadful glassy eyes again. No one liked to follow the dead miller and his living son. Even Grandmother Willoweed felt rather tired, although she recovered on the return journey because she remembered it must be almost tea time. Heavy clouds, some with hard, curdled edges, had gathered in the sky, and the peacocks' harsh cry greeted them as they climbed out of the boat.

That night it became stiflingly hot and not a leaf moved on the trees. It seemed as if a storm were coming; but nothing happened, and the leaves stayed still. Emma was disturbed by Dennis crying and shouting in his sleep; and, although she took him into her own bed and tried to comfort him, he kept starting up and crying that a great fish with the miller's head was trying to devour him. And so the night passed.

CHAPTER VIII

E BIN WALKED under a sticky yellow sky. It seemed
as if there was no air, and the villagers talked together in tired little groups. He stopped when he
reached the bridge, and gazed down at the water; but
that looked yellow and tired too. He had slept little
during the night because the heat in his attic under
the leads had been unbearable, and, when at last he
had managed to doze off, he had been disturbed by
Dennis's cries.

Although it was so stifling, it was only nine o'clock.
From the bridge Ebin watched the little shops opening
and their blinds being drawn up, and the groups of
women parting as they went into various shops. While
he was standing there, the butcher came to the bridge.
He was wearing his straw hat on the back of his head,
and had apparently come to sharpen his knives on the
stone wall. When he had laid the knives across the
wall he stood looking down at them in a vacant way.
Ebin noticed that his swollen fingers were absent-
mindedly plucking at his striped apron. He also
noticed how red and hot the man looked, and remem-

bered he had been seriously ill with some internal trouble recently. As he watched, the butcher's actions became more and more strange. He moved in an odd jerky manner, and appeared to be talking to himself. Then he seemed to have convulsions in his legs, almost as if he was about to do some odd dance, and there was something horribly pathetic about it. His head lolled and rolled on his thick neck, and his eyes stared out from that red moon of a face in a sad bewildered way. Then he picked up a knife with a trembling, bloated hand and suddenly started to sharpen it as if he was in a frenzy, muttering to himself all the time. Ebin thought, 'He is going to have a fit. What can I do? I know his hat will fall off.' Somehow the idea of the butcher's hat falling off seemed a terrible thing. Then the shouting started, that appalling shouting started, and all the time the shining knife was dashing backward and forward over the stone. Dreadful tormented words came pouring out, and Ebin longed to escape from them but dared not move, he couldn't move a step his terror was so great. Mingled with the shouting there were women's screams. Some of them ran into the nearest shop, and he heard them bolt the door and felt he was alone with his terror.

The shouting and sharpening stopped suddenly, and there was only the sound of water rushing through the weir. The butcher was looking at his knife with a look of amazement, as if he had never seen it before and had no idea how it had come into his hand. Then suddenly he began to bellow like some poor bewildered bull, waved his knife as if attacking an in-

visible enemy, and staggered about the bridge. Somehow Ebin managed to crawl away on all fours along
the side of the wall. His mouth wouldn't close and his
saliva dribbled on to the dust, and he imagined he
could smell blood. The bellows abuptly ceased and
turned to strange gurgles. Ebin looked back over his
shoulder and saw the butcher standing swaying gently
on his feet. Suddenly with a swift movement he sliced
his throat right across like a great smile. Ebin closed his
eyes and heard the sound of the huge body falling.
When he looked again the butcher was lying in his
own blood, which had already congealed in places and
resembled raw liver.

Ebin managed to get to his feet, and he stood
trembling with one arm over his eyes. Then he heard
men's voices, and someone led him away to the White
Lion, which stood at the foot of the bridge. They took
him into the billiard room, and laid him on one of the
long, red plush seats.

"No, there is blood on it, take me away," he managed to whisper. They poured whisky down his throat,
and someone tried to fan him with a calendar they
tore from the wall. Flies buzzed against the windows.
The whisky revived him and he struggled to his feet;
but he was gently pushed back on to the sofa.

"You had better stay here a bit, sir, until the Doctor has seen you," said the sympathetic landlady.

"Good God! I'm not cut, am I?" and Ebin hurriedly
examined himself for signs of wounds.

"No but you've had a nasty shock, sir," she reassured him in her soothing voice. "That poor butcher,

whatever possessed him to do a thing like that?"

"It must be the sultry weather," said the man who had helped him to the White Lion, "it's making us all balmy, that's what it's doing. I had terrible dreams myself last night," and the man's lips quivered with the memory of the horror of the night, "and the pains in my stomach have been cruel!"

Ebin looked at him with dismay. Surely he wasn't going mad too. Then he heard Doctor Hatt's voice and felt safe. The doctor entered the billiard room, looking even graver than usual. He gave Ebin a brief examination, pronounced him none the worse for his experience, and offered to drive him home in his new yellow motor-car, which was standing outside the public house; but Ebin did not want to be taken home. He did not feel up to the devastating questions his mother would fire at him when he returned.

"Well, then, you had better come home with me," the doctor said; and they climbed into the high, open car.

At any other time Ebin would have been delighted to drive through the village in the snorting yellow monster; but now he felt too shaken to care. He glanced at the spot on the bridge where he had seen the butcher lying. There was no butcher, no blood, just some yellow sand.

"I suppose the poor chap's dead?" he whispered.

"Yes, as dead as a door nail. I can't understand it; but I hope to God there won't be any more cases. It may be the heat, or it may be some kind of poison has got into the water. I'd better go straight on to the

Medical Officer of Health and arrange to have the water analysed."

Francis Hatt stopped the car outside his own house, and told Ebin to go inside and wait for him. He didn't know how long he would be.

"Ask my old housekeeper to give you some coffee —and the dispenser's there—she'll look after you."

Ebin drank coffee with the dispenser. She was a nice girl, but dull and heavy, like underdone pork. He did not tell her about the butcher's dreadful end, although he could think of nothing else. The words would not come into his mouth; he could almost feel them locked in his chest like a great lump. When the girl had gone back to her duties, he restlessly walked up and down the drawing-room, and suddenly noticed a typewriter and a stack of papers laid out on a table inlaid with marquetry. It looked so unsuitable—a typewriter on that elaborate table—and was a sure sign that Mrs. Hatt was no longer there. The neatly arranged magazines had gone from their usual table; the large bowls of flowers were there no more; even the books on the shelves had changed. It was the first time Ebin realized that Mrs. Hatt was gone for ever and that kind and bustling figure would not appear in her chintzy drawing-room any more.

He tried to concentrate on thoughts of Mrs. Hatt; but it was always the butcher he was really thinking about. He sat down at the table and started experimenting with the typewriter. It was a more modern machine than his own, and moved easily to his touch. He looked at the words he had typed: "The butcher's

throat looked like a smile when he had finished with
it."

He swore and pulled the paper out of the machine
and was about to throw it in the wastepaper-basket;
but suddenly he stopped, and started staring at it as
if he had never seen a piece of paper before.

Then he slowly ripped it into small pieces, placed
a fresh sheet of paper in the typewriter and started to
type again as if in a frenzy.

The dispenser came in to see who could be clattering away like that on the doctor's machine; but Ebin
never noticed her, so she went away again. The old
housekeeper came to ask if he was staying to lunch,
but received no reply. He just continued his furious
typing, and the small bell of the machine clanged
away like a miniature fire engine.

In less than an hour he had finished his typing. He
pinned the sheets together without reading them,
folded them across, and put them in his breast-pocket.
Then he went into Doctor Hatt's dining room and
helped himself to two glasses of sherry. Fortified by
the sherry, he returned to the drawing-room and made
a telephone call to London. It was a long call, and he
had only just replaced the receiver when Doctor Hatt
returned. The doctor thought his friend seemed rather
exhilarated; but put it down to the sherry he had
obviously been drinking.

CHAPTER IX

THE FOLLOWING day the people in the village who subscribed to *The Daily Courier* were surprised to see a leading article headed "Mad Village", giving a lurid description of the last few minutes of the butcher's life and a not quite so lurid description of the miller's end. The article ended with the words, "The inhabitants of this remote village are asking each other 'Who will be smitten by this fatal madness next?'"

This article caused a panic in the village. Already there was another case of violent madness. The victim this time was the man who had helped Ebin Willoweed on the bridge—the man who had complained of nightmares. He lay screaming in his bed and his two brothers had to hold him down. They had tried drugs; they only acted for a short period and then he would start up in bed again yelling that monsters were trying to devour him and that he was a wicked sinner. People gathered outside his cottage on the Broom Road. The cries made their blood run cold, they said, and they did not ask each other "Who's next?" because they had already decided it would be Ebin Willoweed. It must be catching, they said, as they moved a little further from the cottage. Notices appeared in prominent places saying, "Do not Drink Water Unless It has Been Boiled,"—"Trying to pretend it's the water when we know it's the microbes," they muttered. That evening reporters from two newspapers appeared in the village, asking questions and generally prying. They stayed at the "White Lion."

Francis Hatt and the Medical Officer of Health were furious when they read the article in *The Daily Courier*. Francis suspected Ebin Willoweed the moment he read it. It could have only been written by an eye-witness; also he remembered *The Daily Courier* was the newspaper from which Ebin had been dismissed when he first returned to his mother's house years ago. At lunch the previous day Ebin had muttered something about a 'phone call and had reluctantly offered him half-a-crown, which he had refused at the time and now regretted. He was not free now to attack Ebin with his disgraceful behaviour, as the poor demented man on the Broom Road was taking a considerable amount of his time and there were several other patients, mostly suffering from internal trouble, to be attended to, besides frequent discussions with the Medical Officer of Health. They decided to engage a temporary assistant, and a young man from London who had been specialising in brain diseases was on his way to the village. 'But I expect the whole thing will be over by the time he arrives,' the Medical Officer observed.

The assistant—Philip Andrew—arrived the next day, and by that time there were two more cases of the madness, two unrelated children. Their illness had started with stomach trouble; but, when they had almost recovered, their brains became affected. They moaned and shouted, and screamed that terrible monsters were pursuing them, and they clung to their parents in terror. Their poor little legs were drawn up to their stomachs by violent pains, and they frequently vomited. The man who lived on the Broom Road appeared to be recovering, although he was very weak and could take little nourishment and still suffered from hallucinations and insomnia.

There was a joint inquest on the miller and the butcher. It was held at the Assembly Rooms and Ebin was one of the chief witnesses. It was noticed that when he was not giving evidence he was scribbling away on a small pad on his knees. The other journalists were scribbling too. The doctors frowned on them for bringing unwelcome publicity and causing alarm in the village. When the inquest was over, Francis Hatt asked his old friend why he was doing this and pointed out the harm he had done and ended with "Can't you see the village is almost on the verge of mass hysteria?"— and then he regretted the words in case they were scribbled down too. Ebin looked bewildered and hurt and said he had to do it: he couldn't have stopped himself writing the first article; it just came pouring out as if it was writing itself and then, when it was finished, it seemed a pity to waste it. And *The Courier* had been really pleased with it, and wanted anything he could write about the epidemic.

"Francis, you can't think what it is like to be earning money after all these years. To be working again. Do you know I keep touching wood—and it has to be real wood, not painted. The end of the pencil does quite well. I haven't told my mother yet because I know somehow she would put a stop to it; you see, she likes to have me under her thumb. Francis, I'm sorry about it causing panic in the village, but it would have leaked out eventually; this inquest would have drawn attention to it, for one thing!" And the doctor had to agree that this was true, and suddenly gave Ebin one of his dazzling smiles, and they left the assembly rooms together.

Grandmother Willoweed sat in the morning-room eating a honeycomb out of a bowl on her lap. As she licked the wooden frame with her tongue, she bitterly regretted the day she had announced that she would not cross ground that was not her property. At the time she had wondered if she was making a mistake; but it had appeared such a grand gesture and it had seemed unlikely then that she would ever particularly wish to enter the village again. She had a very good view of the main street from the bootroom window with its coloured window-panes of glass. She spent many an amusing half-hour in there with the goloshes and old black boots for company.

But now she felt unhappy. For one thing the honey had become mixed up in her chins and she felt miserably sticky; and she was disturbed by Ebin's behaviour since the catastrophe of the butcher. He had told her

so little about it, in fact he had hardly spoken to her
for days and had become strangely independent, sitting up in his room typing away; now he had been
asked to attend the inquest, and when he returned
would he tell his mother anything about it? she wondered. He was undoubtedly becoming conceited and
out of hand. The old lady picked some beeswax out of
her teeth as she pondered on ways of putting her son
in his place and brightened up a little when she decided to put the maids on to spring cleaning his room.
He couldn't sit up there in haughty isolation under
those conditions. She chuckled to herself and felt
happier. But if only she had been free to wander in
the village and hear the screams coming out of cottage
windows and perhaps even help nurse one of the unfortunate afflicted. She would dearly love to see someone who believed they were being pursued by monsters. So far there had only been five cases, but there
would be more; she was confident there would be
more. One of the maids might become a victim, or
even Old Ives. The thought of Old Ives being devoured
by imaginary monsters cheered her up considerably,
and she trotted off to the potting-shed to see if he
looked at all queer; but she found him looking very
well, sorting out some seeds he had been drying. She
wasn't very pleased with the way he looked at her
and asked how she was feeling.

It was Norah's afternoon off, and she was wearing
her shiny new blue dress to visit Fig's mother; and
she knew that if he was free in time Fig would see
her home. He would not say very much except to re-

mark on the crops as they passed them in the fields;
but he would take her arm, and she would be filled
with pride and happiness. It was an acknowledged
fact now in the village that they were walking out. It
had been one of the chief topics of conversation, combined with the doctor's yellow car; but now the only
subject of interest seemed to be the madness that had
descended upon them. As Nora passed the Assembly
Rooms, the people who had attended the inquest
surged out into the street; and then, when she crossed
the bridge she passed the spot where the poor butcher
had committed suicide and saw the sand which still
covered his blood. When she reached the cottage, Mrs.
Fig, as the village layer-out, could talk of nothing
else.

"Mind you, I love a beautiful corpse as much as
anyone; but there is something about a suicide,
especially one with his throat cut!" she chattered in
her sad little voice, and Norah felt that, even if Fig
saw her home, the afternoon was ruined.

Eunice at Willoweed House was glad Norah was
out of the way and she could lie on their bed and feel
sick and grieve for herself. She had been very sick in
the sink that morning—fortunately before Norah came
down—and she thought she knew why she felt this
way. She remembered the afternoon in the hayfield
and another evening in an orchard when the blossom
was still on the apple trees,—and now little apples
had already formed. "And I know what has formed inside me" the poor girl cried, "it's a baby as sure as fate";
and she felt her breasts and already they seemed to be

enlarged. Then she put her hand on her stomach; but that remained quite flat. Slightly reassured she whispered, "Please God, don't let me have a baby, even if I deserve one, don't let it come." She remembered her mother in her coffin with the little waxen baby lying beside her,— and Norah had cried and called it a poor little thing, but she had hated it because it had killed her mother. Perhaps she would die too if she had a baby; 'but I'm young and I don't want to die yet. Oh, why is it so hard to be good when you are young?' she asked herself.

She left the bed and sat on the window-sill; and through the fir trees she could see glimpses of the village street and remembered how she had watched from that window so often just to get a sight of the top of Joe's cap as he drove past with the hay cart. And sometimes on Sunday she had seen him pushing his ailing wife in a borrowed wicker bath-chair. She could tell he was shy of pushing the chair, because he only used one hand and kept laughing and joking with his wife in a self-conscious manner. But it was kind of him to take his wife out like that—he was a kind man —but his kindness could be little help to her now.

Emma had taken the children on the river, and they had been fishing with the grubs from a wasp's nest Ives had given them. They ate cherries from a basket as they fished, and spat the stones into the water and watched their progress out of sight. "Perhaps even the cherries are contaminated," thought Emma, "but they wouldn't have enjoyed them if they had been boiled first." Since she had heard of the two children in the

village who were suffering from the madness Emma
had been in an agony of mind in case it came to Hattie
and Dennis. Dennis in particular, who she loved so
dearly and who was so dependent upon her. Although
Hattie was younger, she was such a cheerful, independent child, Emma had not such strong feelings for her;
she was her father's favourite, and Emma almost hated
her father and was disgusted and terrified of her
grandmother. The only person she had to love was
Dennis—and the dim lovers of her imagination.

That evening the baker's wife ran down the village
street in a tattered pink nightgown. She screamed as
she ran.

CHAPTER X

THE BAKER and old Toby pursued the demented woman through the village street; but the baker was small and Toby old and she kept far ahead of them, swearing and shouting as she ran. All day she had been behaving strangely, saying she had pains in her stomach, and then drinking and muttering to herself and vomiting. Eventually the baker had persuaded her to go to bed and she had seemed a little calmer, so the worried man returned to his baking of funeral meats and rye bread, for the great joint funeral for the butcher and miller, which was taking place the following day. Toby was standing by his master admiring an enormous pie he was painting with egg yoke when the screams started, and the men exchanged startled glances and ran to the bakery door just in time to see a figure in a pink nightdress running through the open front door. The baker made a grab at his wife who gave him a great push and shouted, "You are the Devil —you bloody devil!" and rushed away leaving part of her nightgown in his hand. Toby helped the baker from the ground and they both ran after the yelling

woman, who leapt and staggered through the village,
as if she was on wires. People screamed and ran into
their houses. Others put their heads out of windows;
children started to cry. But no one came to the baker's
aid. When she reached the bridge she stopped for a
moment by the "White Lion", where only yesterday she
had been drinking and laughing with the journalists.
One of these journalists was standing by the swing
doors of the saloon bar; and he took one startled look
at the wild and terrible woman and ran into the closet
and locked the door. She stood tottering and put her
hands to her stomach and started to retch; then she
saw her husband and Toby bearing down on her and
yelled in a dreadful deep voice, "Leave me alone, you
devils! Oh, leave me alone!" She lurched off down the
street towards Willoweed house. When she reached
the huge green back-gates she clawed at them like a
demented animal, and suddenly they burst open and
she staggered into the yard.

The white cat which had happily been playing with
a leaf rushed away and tore up a trunk of a beech tree
and, as the baker came running into the yard, leapt to
a branch, missed and fell. It fell on the unfortunate
screaming woman below and clawed her bare
shoulders. A look of such demented horror came over
her face; then her jaws began to clamp and she fell
to the ground in a fit with the cat below her. The husband, followed by the old, scarred man, stood at the
gates and saw her long white legs writhing; and then
she was quite still. The baker seemed dazed, stumbled
to her assistance; but there was little he could do except

send Toby for the doctor. He took off his apron to make some kind of pillow for the poor creature's head and tried to pull the torn nightgown to cover the still legs; and he carefully wiped the foam from her lips with his floury handkerchief. While he was looking hopefully at the house windows and wondering if anyone would come to his assistance, Norah came running from the kitchen crying.

"Oh, Mr. Emblyn, I'll come and help you in a moment; but my sister has fainted. She saw it all from the window and is that shocked. Oh, dear!" And the girl ran back to her unconscious sister lying on the stone kitchen floor. Then there was a sound of stumping boots and Grandmother Willoweed appeared in the yard and exclaimed, "Good God! Whatever is all this? Is the woman drunk?"

The overwhelmed baker tried to give an account of what had happened, which was difficult because the old lady constantly interrupted him, and he had difficulty with the ear trumpet. He ended his muddled explanations with, "Oh, ma'm, if only I could have a blanket for my poor wife, she feels so strangely cold."

"Dead most likely!" she replied, shaking out her ear trumpet. "But she needs a blanket to cover up those shocking legs. My son had better help you carry her into the house."

She eyed the dazzling and shapely legs with sullen disfavour and shouted to Norah when she appeared again from the kitchen, "Fetch a blanket and the Master, the blanket first and use one from your own bed."

Ebin arrived before the blanket and stood staring in appalled horror at the beautiful body and coarse face of his old mistress. He was filled with pity and disgust. "How could I have ever touched her?" he thought; but he helped her husband carry her to the kitchen with the utmost care. As she was lifted from the ground the bloodstained body of the squashed cat was revealed.

"That woman has killed my cat," the old woman declared, as she examined the pitiful little body; and she noted with interest that one eye had been squashed right out of its head, while the other remained almost normal.

"Quite remarkable!" she said as she trod purposefully towards the kitchen.

The baker's wife lay on the kitchen table, still and dead. She would no longer prance down the village street in transparent blouses, or lie beneath the willow trees on the river bank on summer afternoons. Doctor Hatt came and made arrangements for the body to be taken to hospital for a post mortem; and now they were waiting for the horse drawn ambulance to arrive. The red kitchen curtains were drawn across the windows, and the corpse was covered by a sheet—which Grandmother Willoweed pulled down now and then to have another look at the dead face.

"Did you know her hair was dyed, Norah?" she asked the terrified maid, whose trembling hands were plucking a chicken. The girl kept her back turned towards the table and envied Eunice, safe in her bedroom on the doctor's orders—but why had he told her to call at the surgery the following day for an examination? 'And bring your sister with you,' he had said. Did he think she was suffering from the madness? she wondered, but it was enough to make a girl faint seeing a mad woman going on like that. He had given her something to make her sleep; but perhaps that was to keep the madness at bay. Norah could bear it no longer and left the half plucked chicken to creep upstairs and look at her sleeping sister. She felt her brow, and it was cool; and she looked so pretty and peaceful lying there in her deep sleep. Norah was reassured and returned to the kitchen. Grandmother Willoweed was there again hovering about the dead woman.

"Foolish girl," she grumbled, "leaving the chicken like that, the cat might have got it."

"There isn't a cat any more," said Norah sadly. She had been fond of that little white cat.

"No more there is," the old woman replied thoughtfully. "The baker will have to take something off his bill. It was quite a valuable cat, and now his wife has killed it. I must speak to him about it when he comes to collect her."

CHAPTER XI

Norah and Eunice sat in Doctor Hatt's waiting room. They wore their white cotton gloves and felt ill at ease. Eunice said nothing and gazed out of the window with unseeing eyes; but Norah talked to a fat woman who was worried by flatulence and to a small boy on his own who was obviously suffering from mumps. Someone had left a copy of *The Daily Courier* on the table, and on the front page there was an article headed, 'Baker's Wife Runs Amok.' Norah turned her eyes away; but the woman next to her seized the newspaper and tried to read bits out loud.

"It says here she was a pitiful sight. I'll say she was. And her husband is a very respected man in the village. That is more than his wife was, so he's well rid of her, I say—"

The woman went on and on and Norah tried to give her attention to the little boy. The madness, the madness, you couldn't get away from it. She glanced at Eunice; but there was no sign of any madness there, although she was strangely quiet and sulky and had been so for days.

"There's the funeral bells," the woman exclaimed, "I'd have dearly loved to have gone to that funeral if it hadn't been for my wind," and she listened enraptured to the sad tolling of the bells.

Doctor Hatt was standing at the surgery door saying, "I can see you now, Eunice," and he smiled at the girls kindly. They followed him into the ether-smelling surgery and stood close together by the door.

"Now, Eunice," he said, "I shall have to give you a thorough examination. You must take your clothes off behind that screen, and then I shall want you to lie on the couch." They looked at the black, shiny couch with a strip of white running down the centre.

Twenty minutes later the girls were walking down the village street, and they could still hear the funeral bell tolling in their ears although it had ceased some time ago. Eunice held on to her sister's arm; but they did not speak to each other.

They did not speak until they had reached the privacy of their bedroom, and then Eunice sat on their bed and cried, "Oh, Norah, what am I to do, it's . . . Joe Lott's baby and he can't marry me. Norah, don't be cross with me."

She held her head in her hands and large tears rolled down her pink cheeks. Norah tried to think what to say or what suggestions to make and at last she said:

"I blame myself. I should have looked after you better. I was so happy with Fig walking out together in the fields and I really think he was coming round to marrying me. But he won't now, not with the disgrace, and all."

Then Eunice cried even more because she had ruined her sister's chance of marriage, and Norah comforted her and they tried to make plans for the future. "I must see Joe just once more to tell him what has happened. I did kind of hint about it the last time I saw him, but he laughed, and said it couldn't be true. Joe was always laughing, that's what made me like him at first; but I don't want him to laugh about the baby, just be kind." And they sat there with their arms around each other until they were disturbed by the harsh voice of their mistress calling up the back stairs, "Come downstairs girls. Don't you know it's after four?"

Ebin Willoweed had telephoned an account of the funeral to *The Courier* from the village post office, and he laughed to himself on his way home thinking how his mother pounced on his articles after breakfast each morning, even reading bits out loud to him, but never suspecting they were written by her own son. He felt guilty when he thought of the dreadful suffering and horror going on around him, which was directly the cause of his happiness and sudden prosperity. Then he thought of his mistress's poor dead body, with its raddled old face, lying out in the yard.

"I won't think of it," he muttered to himself. "They have had their happiness and I've been wretched for years. It's my turn now. Perhaps I shall get the madness next; so I must enjoy the little time I have. Good God, I'm most likely mad now, talking to myself," and he strode through the village in a purposeful manner to prove to himself he wasn't going mad.

While the family were at tea, his mother suddenly attacked him about the children's education and wanted to know why their lessons had abuptly ceased. He had been expecting this, and had indeed been re-hearsing imaginary conversations with his mother on this subject, and to his surprise the discussion went just as he had hoped and he was able to produce his trump card and say that it was time Dennis went to school and he was in a position to pay the fees. "As a matter of fact, I'm thinking of sending him into the Navy later on."

"As a stoker, no doubt," his mother replied. "Any-way you are talking absolute nonsense. You are nothing less than a beggar dependent on my charity, and, if you are counting on any publisher buying one of your trumpery novels, you must be more of a fool than I already believe you to be."

"Now mother, calm yourself." He spoke to her in a mockingly soothing voice. "I've been doing quite well lately. I think the last cheque I paid into my bank yesterday was for ninety-eight pounds, and I shall be paying in another nice little sum in a few days, I ex-pect. You can leave Dennis's school fees quite safely to me, Mother."

"I don't believe it. You are lying. No one would pay you for the rubbish you write." But as she spoke she remembered the sound of the long unused typewriter that had come floating down the stairs to be caught in her ear trumpet. "If you are speaking the truth you can pay . . . you can pay for your keep and for your children . . . all three of them," the old woman spluttered out her words in jerks.

"Well, if that's the position Mother, I think I'll return to London. It will be near my work and most
likely cheaper," and, as he got up to leave the table,
he glanced at his mother and saw she was almost
purple in the face and seemed to be having trouble
with her teeth. Hattie started to laugh but Emma
frowned at her, so she covered her face with her
hands and hoped her grandmother would think she
was crying. The old woman clumped from the room
to adjust her teeth in the pantry, and when she returned the dining-room was empty. She stood there
for a moment gazing at the remains of the tea on the
table and the hastily-pushed-back chairs. Her jaw
started to tremble, and she stood tapping the table
with her short, thick fingers; then she turned away and
slowly climbed the stairs to her room.

Ebin was delighted. It was the first time he had
routed his mother for years, and he had rushed his
family from the room before she returned to spoil his
victory. He suggested taking the children for a walk
to the miser's cottage—a little burnt house, hardly more
than a hut, all deserted in a field. Once in an inventive
mood he had told them it had been an old miser's cottage and that the gold that was hidden there had never
been found, although people had taken down most of
the cottage in their search after the miser's death.
Hattie and Dennis half believed this story and loved
to dig up the flagstones on the floor and pick away at
the charred walls of the cottage for gold and treasure.
For some reason, perhaps because their father had

first told them about the old miser, they felt in honour bound never to go to the cottage without him, and often there were many months between their visits and always more of the cottage had fallen down since they had last been there. This time they were armed with a cork-screw and a long bone-handled nail-file, and with these they attacked the miser's chimney, and after about half an hour's scraping and filing they did manage to take out one brick. They would have been quite content to spend the entire evening taking down the rest of the chimney.

Ebin watched them at first with amusement and he thought, 'I don't care what anyone says, I'm a good chap really. Not many men placed as I am would spend their first earnings for years on their son's education, and here I am in a little broken-down hovel just to give my children amusement. Emma didn't want me to bring them here, — jealous, I suppose. Didn't want the children to walk through the village in case they caught this thing that is about. But you can't coddle them like that; it's making Dennis a damn cissy. Francis Hatt doesn't seem to think this thing is contagious anyway. They haven't found anything wrong with the water yet; so now they are having a shot at the bread, I believe. Might write something for the Courier about that.' As his thoughts rambled on, he leant against the blackened cottage wall, poking the floor with his stick. He noticed the tender young ferns pushing their way between the flagstones. 'A few weeks ago I wouldn't have noticed how beautiful those ferns were in this desolate place. It must be because I'm happier that I see things with new eyes these days.' And he wandered from the cottage and stood looking down the valley, and watched the cows returning from being milked and walking with their graceful walk, gently turning their heads from side to side. 'If only women walked like cows instead of strutting and stamping with their heels they would look a damn sight better,' he thought; but suddenly he became impatient and was tired of the ruined cottage and the children and wanted to be at the White Lion talking to the journalists who were staying there.

The children were by this time extremely dirty and rather tired and did not want to be hustled home. Then, unfortunately, they came to one of the fields filled with the cows their father had so much admired. Dennis was frightened of cows and, when he saw the great beasts tossing their heads adorned with their curling horns, he knew he could never pass them. Even the ones who were grazing kept slashing at flies with their tails in an alarming manner. He stood at the gate and refused to budge while Hattie coaxed him and his father swore, "You bloody little fool, they won't hurt you. If you don't come immediately. I'll leave you here and you'll have to face them all alone!" And that is exactly what did happen. Ebin went on, although both children begged him not to, and he forced Hattie to go with him, which she sulkily did, looking over her shoulder every now and then at the sad little figure standing by the gate. When they had gone out of sight Dennis rushed back to the miser's hovel with the idea of staying there until the following morning, when the farmer would take the offending cows away to be milked. The grimy little ruin had lost its charm and appeared a desolate place to the boy, who sat down on a pile of bricks to wait for the morning, which seemed so far away. When it was almost dark, some enormous flying beetles started a mad and dreadful dance round a may tree with the blossom all dried and brown upon it.

When they reached the bridge, Ebin told Hattie to go home by herself because he wanted to visit the White Lion. He felt depressed and the good esteem in which he had been holding himself had somehow gone. He hoped Dennis would have returned before he did; otherwise there would be great trouble with Emma. And now he kept thinking of the lonely small figure standing by the gate in the dusk. But a country boy afraid of cows — it was too absurd! I shall feel better after a drink, he thought as he tripped into the White Lion. When he left half an hour later he had heard that there were eleven new cases of the strange illness in the village. Also, the dog from the White Lion had died of convulsions.

CHAPTER XII

W HEN EMMA discovered Hattie had returned without Dennis she was rather unjustly angry with
the child. She was not unduly worried because she
thought her father must have returned for Dennis
when he had sent Hattie home by herself. But later
she heard the heavy front gates close and saw Ebin
walking through the dank, tree-lined front garden
alone.

"Where's Dennis?" she demanded.

"Dennis?" her father asked, "Isn't he home yet? I've
just heard there are eleven new cases of this madness,
and, strangely enough, they were all guests at the
funeral; so it must be contagious after all."

"Of course it's contagious," Emma almost
screamed, "and you've taken the children right
through the village and left Dennis alone in some
wretched field. I hope you are the next one to get
the madness, indeed I do!" And she rushed past him
into the street.

Emma hurried through the village. It was already
dusk and lamps were being lit in cottage windows. She

passed the White Lion and heard laughter and voices
and the click of billiard balls coming out, and there
was a smell of beer. She crossed the bridge and entered
the small field which had belonged to the butcher, and
she startled the dreamy sheep waiting to be killed
by the butcher who had already killed himself. The
next field had lately been cut for hay and now was
very green, and horses had been turned into it to
graze. Pontius Pilate — an aged golden hunter who
drew the village cab — followed her hopefully, because she usually brought him sugar lumps; but she
did not notice him as she hurried through the field.
She passed old Toby's cottage, where already the
dahlias were showing high, and she asked the old man
if he had seen Dennis. He looked at her dreamily out
of his sad red eyes and then recognised her.

"No, Miss Willoweed. I haven't seen the boy. Can
I help you find him, do you think, Miss?"

But she refused his help and was afraid of his
scarred face, which she had not seen so close before.

She climbed the hill that led to the ruined hovel,
and, as she came near a cottage with lights showing
from every window, she heard a child's piercing
screams and a woman crying. Then a terrified child
with tousled hair appeared at the window and rattled
the casement; but a man quickly grabbed it and it disappeared from view. But the screams came again.
Emma stood for a moment staring at the cottage in
horror while she tried to summon enough courage to
go to the child's assistance; and, as she stood there, a
man came to the window and tried it to see if it was

firmly closed, and the child's tormented screams arose
again. As the man at the window turned away, Emma
recognised Doctor Hatt's cadaverous face. Startled,
she drew into the shadows, and she realised the demented child she had seen at the window was suffering from the madness.

"Oh, please, God, don't let Dennis get it, and help
that poor child," she found herself praying as she
stumbled in the dusk up the rough hillside path.

It was almost dark when she found Dennis asleep
on the broken stone floor of the hut. He gave a bewildered cry as she gently touched his shoulder, but
was reassured when he heard her voice. Although the
evening was warm, he appeared to be cold and re-
peatedly shivered; so Emma made him run down the
hill to bring back some warmth to his body. They
passed through the field with the cows; but he did not
seem to notice them, although their comfortable
breathing and occasional husky coughs could be
heard in the darkness. When they came to the cottage
where the demented child had screamed, all was still
and there was only a light in one window. The moon
was rising, and there was a beautiful smell of summer
night about. The quietness was suddenly disturbed by
the sound of angry voices and muttered mumblings.

When they came near old Toby's cottage they
could see it was surrounded by people, and a great
rumble of anger seemed to be coming from them and
above it there were shouts for Toby to show himself.

"Come out, you bastard—come out you murderer!"
Then someone shouted, "If you don't come out, we

will burn your house down."

"Yes, burn the bugger," a thin little woman, wearing a man's cloth cap, yelled as she savagely elbowed her way through the crowd.

The miller's son seized a rake from the garden and beat on the door shouting, "You killed my Dad with your filthy bread. Come out you scabby old monster!"

Emma and Dennis stood on the outskirts of the crowd, which had now advanced right up to the cottage, and there was a sound of breaking glass as they beat the windows in with sticks. The enormous dahlias were trodden underfoot.

"Poor old Toby, what can he have done?" Emma asked a scared-looking woman standing near.

"I don't know, I'm sure, miss," she replied, "but I did hear as they say he put poison in the bread and that's the cause of this here illness—or madness, as they call it."

The woman melted into the shadows, and Emma and Dennis cringed against a hedge. Besides the shouting there were other most disturbing sounds like some great malevolent animal snorting and grunting, and there was a stench of evilness and sweating, angry bodies. A man with his shirt all hanging out pushed past Emma, and in the moonlight she could see his face all terrible, with loose lips snarling and saliva pouring down his chin. Shrieks of laughter greeted him when he climbed on the thatched roof and shouted and swore down the chimney. Several men carried lanterns, which they wildly waved above their heads and which made a strange and dancing light. Emma and Dennis crept against the hedge, and, although they were pushed and jostled, they clung to each other and were not parted. They stumbled over two unheeding figures rolling and grunting on the grass, and a woman with her mouth all bleeding pushed them out of her way as she ran yelling towards the village. She battled her way through the mob, and Emma, dragging Dennis, ran in her wake, and suddenly they were free and the crowd and terror were behind them.

As they trailed through the village street they heard the roar of Doctor Hatt's car, and, as it passed them, they saw the doctor was accompanied by the policeman, and Dennis said sleepily, "Look Emma, old Toby will be saved now."

Emma looked over her shoulder at the car as it passed across the bridge and saw that the sky was all lit up and glowing, and knew that they were burning Toby's cottage. She gave Dennis a gentle push, told him to hurry home and get Norah to give him something hot to drink, and rushed back over the bridge. She forgot her recent terror and tiredness and only felt a compelling urge to shield the wretched old man from his persecutors.

She returned to see the cottage blazing. Floating, burning straw from the thatching was starting minor fires all round, and the heat and smoke were terrible. The crowd become subdued and afraid and many were creeping away, some of the men with their coats over their heads, so that they could not be recognised. The policeman had managed to round up a few and was questioning them; but no one appeared to know if Old Toby was still in the cottage. Doctor Hatt tried the door; but although it was burning the bolts still remained firm. The heat and smoke were so intense, he was driven back.

"Is that poor man still in there?" he shouted to the crowd; but there was no reply above the roaring and crackling of the fire. A few men half-heartedly advanced towards the cottage with sticks as if to beat the flames out; but they soon retreated with streaming eyes and glowing red, scorched faces.

Emma ran to the back of the house where it was comparatively clear. She had an idea the old man might have crept out that way and be hiding in his privy among the giant cabbages. It was then that she started to scream—a dreadful penetrating scream on one awful note. They thought it was the old man trapped and burning alive in his house, and Doctor Hatt made one frantic attempt to climb through the tiny broken window; but the size of the window and the heat made it impossible.

The hideous scream continued, and then the dark people with dancing flames on their faces were all around Emma as she stood there among the wilting cabbages. One hand was over her mouth as if to stop the scream and the other was pointing at something crawling on the ground, and as they came nearer it became still and they recognised it as something human. As they bent over the still form, there was a sickening smell of burnt flesh and smouldering cloth still burning. The fierce changing light revealed old

Toby's charred corpse more terrible than he had ever
been in life, and, although the doctor bent over him
in compassion, most of the onlookers staggered away
half fainting and some uncontrollably vomiting.

Someone quite gently led Emma away and helped
her to sit upon a tree trunk away from the heat. There
she stayed vaguely watching the disturbed insects that
madly rushed about its bark and she muttered over
and over again, "He smelt so dreadful, and he
crawled . . ."

Old Toby's body was wrapped in sacks, so recently
used for forcing rhubarb, to prevent the limbs from
falling from the body, and carefully lifted into the
back seat of the doctor's car. As the policeman
climbed into the front seat and the doctor went to
the front of the car to turn the starting handle, several
men sprang forward offering their help. As if from
nowhere Ebin Willoweed suddenly appeared with
notebook in hand and demanding to be told how
Toby's cottage came to be burnt. The doctor pushed
past him without speaking and got into the throbbing
car and drove away; at the same time the horse-drawn
fire engine arrived.

The absence of the policeman and the presence of
the fire engine drew the crowd back, and Ebin went
from one to another trying to get a coherent account
of all that had passed that evening. Eventually he
almost fell over Emma, still sitting on her log staring
at insects. Although surprised to see her, he immediately asked her how much she had seen.

"I want an eye witness account, Emma."

But the only answer he received was, "He smelt dreadful and he crawled . . ."

When he had managed to piece some sort of a story together, he returned for Emma, who had just noticed the crowd had nearly disappeared and the fire was almost out. She stood up feeling quite dazed and somehow managed to follow her father across the moonlit field to the river, where Ebin had moored a boat. Silently they rowed across; but as he tied the boat to the landing stage Ebin said "It's a pity I missed most of it."

"I only wish I'd never returned," Emma thought as she wearily walked towards the house.

Before going to her room she remembered Dennis and went to see if he was safely in bed. A light was shining below his door, and when she entered his room she saw a candle was still burning on his chest-of-drawers and she held it over the sleeping boy. She saw that he had gone to bed without washing, and his hands and face were streaked with black. She smiled for a moment; but then her eyes fell on a half-finished hunk of rye bread and butter and a pot of jam on the chair by his bed. She remembered hearing that the bread had been examined for poisoning, and she flung it through the open window. As she did so she saw the glow across the river from the remains of old Toby's cottage, which was still burning.

CHAPTER XIII

IVES ARRIVED the next morning and was full of the news, and rumours that were circulating in the village. When Grandmother Willoweed heard his excited old voice floating out of the kitchen, she tugged the cord of her huge bell and demanded that Ives should be sent to her immediately. The old man did not like the idea of entering ladies' bedrooms; but he was eager to tell his news and followed Eunice quite docilely. When he entered the room, however, he was so overcome by the smell of camphor combined with peppermint and stuffy old clothes that he couldn't get his breath to speak and there was a dreadful pause, which rather increased the drama of his words when they eventually came.

"Well ma'm, it's like this. Toby that worked for the baker is burnt to a cinder — dead, and the old ladies at Roary Court . . . well, their goat's dead, died in the most terrible convulsions, and one of the old ladies herself is none too well—diarrhoea and hands and feet shaking like a leaf. But that's not all. There are strange policemen and other strangers taking away all the baker's flour and he's in a terrible state; it's almost as if he had the madness himself. And ma'm, there won't be no baking there for many a day. All our bread is coming in carts from over Stratford way. Oh, yes, and I saw Doctor Hatt's man, Mr. Fig, and he says there are seventeen suffering from this poisoning or madness or whatever it be; but they don't seem to be dying, just terrible pains and never a wink of sleep. But Fig's a close one and its more than likely that they are dying like flies."

The old man stopped for lack of breath, and, if Grandmother Willoweed had been able to smile, she would have smiled kindly at him. Instead, she thanked him for his interesting information and told him he was to ask the servants to give him a good breakfast.

"Anything you like, — gammon, kidneys, eggs, separate or all together, just as you fancy. And, while you are about it, you can tell them to bring up my tray; I'm famished."

Emma had slept late, but was disturbed by the old people's voices. She hastened over her washing and dressing; but, before she had finished brushing her long hair, Hattie came sadly into her room with three dead birds she had discovered on the round lawn that came close to the house. One of the birds — a robin — was still warm, and she gave it to Emma and asked if there was a chance that it was not really dead but only in a faint.

"No, I'm afraid it's dead," Emma said as she gently stroked the limp body, "but why three birds should suddenly die on our lawn, I cannot say. There is no

sign of violence and it cannot be thirst so near the
river."

She gave the sad little body back to Hattie, who
suddenly said:

"Oh, I forgot to tell you. Dennis won't get up because he says he's cold."

"Cold? Hattie, why didn't you tell me before instead of showing me those silly birds!" Emma exclaimed as she roughly pushed her sister out of the
way and ran to Dennis' bedroom, while Hattie buried
her dark face on the bird's bodies and wept.

Dennis lay in bed shivering, and complaining that
he felt tired; and Emma, who had had little experience of illness, felt his forehead and, when that
seemed cool against her hand, was reassured. He had
every reason to feel tired after his experiences the
previous evening, she reasoned, and he would be well
enough by lunch time if he was allowed to rest. He refused his breakfast, but drank a glass of hot milk, and
then lay quietly, apparently happy, looking at the
cracks in the ceiling.

"That one's just like Australia with the big bite out,
and there is one in the corner just like Ireland—or it
could be a Teddy bear," he said dreamily to Emma as
she was leaving the room.

At the bakery, Horace Emblyn sat broken-hearted
by his empty flour bins. All his flour had been confis-
cated and condemned, although it was only established
that the rye bread had contained ergot. The previous
evening the medical officer of health, accompanied by
the policeman, had called at the bakery and informed

him that it was the bread that he baked which had poisoned the villagers and caused the madness. He was responsible for his wife's death, the butcher's death, the miller's death, — and perhaps there would be others who would suffer and die through eating the bread he had made with such pleasure. There were seventeen new cases, not very severe as yet, but it was quite likely that some of them would end in death through eating rye bread baked by Horace Emblyn.

"I'm a mass murderer," he thought, as he sat on an empty sack by his empty bins. "There is no good smell of baking bread coming from my ovens because I've caused such dreadful and sinister things to come about. I who have always been gentle and meek and never mis-called my wife for her goings on, and never took birds' eggs as a boy or caught lizards and put them in little boxes to die. I never felt much anger towards any man or struck a blow that I can remember; but I've caused more suffering than any man alive, I shouldn't wonder." And so his thoughts went round under his limp brown hair, and he almost hoped the villagers would mob together and burn him to death as they had Old Toby. The previous evening, after the medical officer of health had left, he had stuffed his mouth with bitter rye flour and tried to choke it down. It was so dry it was impossible to swallow; but he managed to eat a considerable amount by mixing it with water and stuffing it down his throat with his hand. Yet he felt no sign of the burning pains in his stomach, just a dreadful, sick tiredness. He longed to share the pain that he had inflicted; but now there was

no more ergot-contaminated bread or flour for him to
push down his unwilling throat. He left his sack and
wandered round his bakery to sadly examine his
ovens, which were almost cold. He opened the doors
and looked at the awful emptiness inside, and he
examined the empty tins already floured and prepared
to receive their share of dough. In the sink there were
bowls, which had contained sugar-icing of various
colours, waiting to be washed. He noticed a trap with
a crushed mouse spread upon it. There was a bead of
blood upon its mouth and he turned away for a
moment and then forced himself to look at it. Who
was he to turn from a murdered mouse, when he was
responsible for so many deaths? He carefully freed
the stiff little creature and held it in his hand, wondering what to do with it. He put it in a box which had
once contained coloured birthday candles, and placed
some silver leaves on top.

"I must bury you, sometime," he murmured, and
then noticed a speck of blood on his hand. He went
to the sink to wash it away, although he felt it was
not right to do so when he had so much death on him
already. On the window-sill he saw the sun streaming
purple through a bottle of carbolic. He held the hand
with the smear of blood upon it in the purple ray, and
then he took the bottle and uncorked it, and the fierce,
clean smell came out.

The baker knelt on the stone floor and whispered,
"Please God, forgive me; but let me suffer for ever
and ever." Then he emptied as much of the contents
of the bottle as he could before he fell choking to the

ground, consumed by burning pains more terrible than any that had been suffered in that village.

* * * *

During the afternoon Ives went to Grandmother Willoweed, who was sunning herself in a basket chair on the top path.

"Baker's dead, ma'm," he shouted down her trumpet, "and Mrs. Fig's got the madness or else it's the D.T's., and the little old peacock's dead too; we haven't got one now. But my ducks is alright," and he turned away towards the river to make sure this was still so.

CHAPTER XIV

DENNIS CRIED that he was hot, and then said cold waves were coming over him, and Emma sat by his bed and almost cried too. Late in the afternoon she asked her grandmother to send for the doctor; but the old lady said she was sure he was being tiresome. She did consent to take his temperature and clumped off to her bedroom to find the thermometer, an object seldom used in Willoweed House. It was eventually discovered in a shoe box with Dennis's birth certificate and a receipt for calves' feet jelly. The grandmother was not quite sure how it worked and shook it about franticly for about five minutes before putting it in Dennis's mouth. He asked, "Will it hurt dreadfully?" and, when at last it was in his mouth, was surprised that nothing happened except that it tasted of dust. After about ten minutes it was taken out with great ceremony; but then there was the difficulty of reading it. "There is a mark for normal somewhere, but I can't see it. If the boy's really ill the quicksilver shows above that!" They both peered at the thermometer and at last Emma discovered the silver line ended at 96·8, well below normal, and they were both reassured; he really must be in very good health to have a temperature as low as that.

"I think you are just pretending," Grandmother Willoweed said rather crossly as she swept from the room, holding the thermometer before her like a wand and looking very like the bad fairy in a pantomime. Dennis felt he was in disgrace for feigning illness, and as he lay shivering in bed said, "All the same, Emma, if being extra well feels like this, it isn't very pleasant. I'd rather be ill any day."

In the scullery Norah was preparing the vegetables for the evening meal, and Eunice sat huddled up on a three-legged stool by the copper.

"Do you know what day it is, Norah?" she asked in a depressed voice.

"I can't say I do," her sister replied as she cut an over-large new potato in half.

"Well, it's the 22nd of June, and there is a great Coronation going on all over England except here, where we are so downhearted. King George will be wearing his crown today and the flags will be waving in the wind and people drinking out of their Coronation mugs. Don't you remember we were going to drive in the village in decorated carts?"

"I can't remember anyone asking me to go in a decorated cart; but they may have wanted you because you're so pretty. But fancy forgetting all about it. Fig was telling me that some people from the village were going all the way to Evesham to celebrate and they were going into the gardens there to make merry under a great arch which is really the jaw bone of a whale. Oh, I would have liked to have gone; but Fig's mother is ill now and things are so sad."

"Yes, that's true," her sister replied dolefully, "and you can't think how my stomach hurts now I'm having a baby."

When Emma went to bed that night she could see fireworks in the distance, and she watched them for a few moments until she remembered the dreadful burning of Old Toby's cottage.   She hurried to bed, and was just drifting into sleep when she heard Dennis calling her. She stumbled out into the darkness, ran to his room and found him crying that he couldn't sleep and that his insides were on fire. She tried to soothe him before she went down to the deserted kitchens and warmed him milk over an oil stove; but it was almost cold before she could get him to drink it. All through the night the little boy tossed and turned and cried about the burning pains inside him. And then the sheets became dirty, and Emma had to change them and hide the dirty ones so that her grandmother would not be angry. When at last it was dawn and the birds began to sing, they hoped the terrible night was over; but it was hardly four o'clock and there were several more frightful hours to be lived through.

At last Emma heard one of the maids wrestling with the kitchen range, and she went down to find a grey-faced Norah wearing a coat over her flannel night-gown.

"Excuse me being like this, Miss, but I'm so worried about my sister. She's been ill all night with burning pains and no sleep at all. Oh, it's been so dreadful to watch her suffering so, and there is little I can do to ease her. It is the bread poisoning, I know it is!"

"Norah, that is just how Dennis has been. I've been up with him all the night; but he's no better. Do come and look at him and tell me what you think."

The two girls went to Dennis's room and examined the little boy, who certainly looked extremely ill in the bright morning light. His face was grey, and he was bathed in perspiration and seemed hardly conscious; and, although his eyes were open, they did not appear to focus properly. Norah was shocked at the change in the child and said the doctor should be sent for immediately.

"But Norah, I'm sure my grandmother will be angry if I call in the doctor without her permission; and if I wake her up she will be even more angry. I'm so tired, I can't bear one of her scenes. Do you think Father would come and look at Dennis? And then he might send for the doctor or even go for him himself. Norah, do go and tell him how ill Dennis is. He will believe it more serious if it comes from you."

So Norah called Ebin Willoweed, and after a considerable amount of grumbling he consented to come and look at his son. When he did he could hardly believe that wan little figure was Dennis. Even as he watched the boy suddenly doubled up in the bed and cried in a weak, small voice that he was burning, and in his pain he tried to sit up, but fell back fainting.

"Good God!" his father cried, "Dennis are you alright, Dennis?" and he caught one clammy little arm and almost shook him. As soon as he showed a sign of consciousness, Ebin dressed and rushed from the house to fetch Doctor Hatt. On the way there he kept remembering the many times he had been impatient, and, worse still, so bullying, with Dennis. He always regretted it later and would determine to be kinder to the boy; but it never lasted. He remembered with shame how he used to lose his temper when he was teaching him to swim and how he had banged his hands with a paddle when he tried to hold on to the boat. He could almost see the hands now, small and shaking and blue with cold, clutching the varnished wood of the boat. "I expect the boy almost hates me," he thought dejectedly, as he rang the brass bell with "Day" engraved on it.

Doctor Hatt came to Willoweed House unshaven and hollow-eyed. He pronounced Dennis and Eunice both to be suffering from ergot poisoning; but with Dennis the attack was more severe. He suggested that a nurse should be sent for immediately; and, before night came again, a Nurse Fenwick with a black moustache was installed and the whole house was in a state of upheaval. Grandmother Willoweed was overcome by her grandson's horrifying illness and spent hours in her room brewing disgusting concoctions which she thought would help the boy. The nurse discovered her trying to put cut-up black threads down the child's throat, which she insisted were a cure for worms and other foreign bodies in the stomach. She also boiled a mouse in an eggshell, and declared it was an unfailing cure for whooping cough and most likely to cure other more unusual afflictions. She bitterly resented the nurse; but she even more resented Eunice's illness at such an inconvenient time, and instead of getting extra help from the village made Norah do the work of two as well as looking after her sister. From time to time the angry old face would appear round Eunice's door and she would shout, "Get up girl, get up you lazy slut. There is nothing wrong with you, you are not even screaming!" Poor Eunice would lie there bathed in pain and perspiration, and in terror in case the doctor told her tormentor her secret and she would be sent home to an angry father with her illness and disgrace upon her. She lay in her tumbled bed limp and wan, and, when the burning pains seemed to be consuming her, she felt it was the punishment for her sin and she was sure she was dying. But when the pains were not so fierce she begged her sister to bring Joe to see her. "Just to see him once more so that I can remember him when I'm lonely in my grave," she entreated. But Norah knew it would be impossible to smuggle Joe into the house and up the back staircase into her sister's bedroom, and in any case it would be most improper. Even if it was Eunice's dying wish, she could not bring herself to encourage such goings on. Then, when Norah was preparing the breakfast, she heard screams coming from above and left the bacon to burn and ran to her sister's aid, expecting to find the madness had started and that she would do herself some injury. In a panic she remembered she had left the windows open to air the room. There was

Eunice crouched at one end of the bed with an expression of horror on her face, and when she saw Norah she pointed to the bed and said, "Look there's blood everywhere!"

"Yes, yes, dear, come and lie down," she said soothingly; and then she saw that it was indeed true and the sheets were all blood-stained and terrible. For a moment she thought Eunice was about to die; and then she remembered her condition and hoped it was only a miscarriage, and she was able to calm the terrified girl. She changed the sheets and made her comfortable and promised she would bring the doctor to her as soon as he came. She was hiding the stained sheets in a closet when Grandmother Willoweed stumped past the door muttering about burning bacon. Then they heard her footsteps pass again and she returned to her room.

When Doctor Hatt came to the house he examined Eunice and pronounced that she had suffered a miscarriage. Norah begged him not to tell the old lady, and he muttered something about it 'not being necessary' and went to join his assistant Philip Andrew, who was already waiting for him in Dennis's bedroom.

CHAPTER XV

THE YOUNG doctor stood looking down at the almost unconscious Dennis, who lay quite still except for a trembling of the hands. Emma sat beside him so exhausted she did not hear him enter the room and was startled when he asked her to fetch the nurse. She looked at him with her heavy brown eyes, too large for her narrow, white, dreaming face. "She is like an El Greco Madonna," he thought, "except for the hair; but, if that was covered with blue drapery,—but then it's so beautiful. She is perfect as she is." He collected himself and said:

"Miss Willoweed, the nurse, if you tell the nurse Doctor Hatt is here to see your brother—"

"Oh yes, of course, you are one of the doctors. I'll tell the nurse," and she crept from the dark little room as Doctor Hatt entered it.

"That poor girl is taking her brother's illness very badly," he said as he closed the door preparatory to telling his assistant about Eunice's miscarriage.

"I'll have to make a report; but there is no need to let the old lady know. The nurse can keep an eye on her. Ah, here she is!"

The nurse entered the room with a rustle of starch and her mouth coyly smiling under her moustache, and the examination of Dennis began.

When the two doctors left the room they found Ebin Willoweed standing on the landing under some stags' horns, biting his nails. He looked at their grave faces and followed them downstairs with a dreadful sinking of his heart. Francis Hatt was surprised to observe how acutely his friend was suffering from his boy's illness and put his hand on his arm for a moment as he said, "I'm afraid he's very ill indeed, and I can give you little hope. Would you be willing to send him to hospital, where I think he would stand a better chance?"

But Ebin would not agree to Dennis being sent to hospital, and shook the doctor's hand from his arm and hurried upstairs to see his son for himself. The nurse was just leaving the room as he entered and she pushed past him rather impatiently, but was punished for her rudeness by meeting Grandmother Willoweed on the landing. The old woman was in a dreadful state because she thought she could hear a death-watch beetle in her wardrobe; and she insisted on the nurse coming to listen. The nurse turned down her mouth at the evil-smelling room, and stood stiffly as the old woman bent by the cupboard straining to hear through her ear trumpet.

"It's a mouse," she declared crossly. "Don't you know a mouse when you hear one? You should get a trap or cat and get rid of the disgusting creature."

"But my cat's dead," wailed the old woman, "that wicked woman the baker's wife squashed it, and now I have to have mice in my room. It's too unjust!"

The nurse turned and left the room, but, suddenly remembering that Grandmother Willoweed would be the one to pay her, for her services, she opened the door a chink and shouted, "Such a pity about your cat!"

As the doctors left the house together they saw Norah and Fig talking. He had just told Norah that his mother had died in a muscular spasm which followed a violent attack of delirium, and he seemed greatly distressed at losing his disreputable parent. 'How strange that he should grieve for that dirty old woman!' thought Norah. "But he was a good son, and they say good sons make even better husbands." So she said suitably comforting words to him, hoping that he would not know they were insincere.

As the day passed Dennis grew worse, and hallucinations came to him in the form of dreadful animals and strange fires. The poor child's cries could be heard through the house, and Grandmother Willoweed became hysterical and thought the end of the world had come and it was Revelations that were happening. Hattie and her father went to the river and sat in one of the moored boats, two unhappy humped figures in the sun. The nurse turned Emma from the room; but she sat under her brother's window in the dark front garden and leant against the ivy-covered walls that smelt of bitter dust. She listened to her brother's terrified cries, and even when they ceased they seemed to

echo in her head. She saw the doctors come again
through the green gates and later heard their voices
droning from the window above, and she heard the
nurse's bright little laugh and then Dennis's shrill
voice, high and strained, describing some fabulous
vision. She sat so still a baby robin, brown and very
round, settled on her shoe and gave a plaintive chirp
and she shook her foot as she said, "Go away, you
beastly bird;" for she remembered the maids telling
her that birds, usually robins, came into the house
when death was expected. Once old Ives had told
her that, when his young brother was dying, a dove
with one broken wing had come into the kitchen and
flown about the dresser, breaking the blue plates, and
his father had wrung its neck.

It began to grow dark, and Ebin and Hattie left the
boat and crept back to the house. In the dusky hall
the clock sounded loudly in the stillness; but upstairs
there was the sound of great snores from Grandmother Willoweed, who had been drugged without
her knowledge. Ebin paused by his son's door and
then opened it a little way, half dreading what he
would see; but all he saw was Dennis lying very still
and Philip Andrews intently watching beside him.

"How is he?" he asked in a husky whisper.

"Well it's difficult to say," the young doctor
answered. "He's quieter now; but he's very exhausted
and had a form of epileptiform convulsions about an
hour ago. If he gets through this night, I think the
worst will be over. Anyway, Doctor Hatt is coming
along soon and will stay most of the night with him.

The nurse is having a bit of a rest—and, by the way, I hope you don't mind, but we had to give your mother a little something to quieten her; she had got in rather a state!"

"Oh, no, of course not. I only wish you would do it more often."

Ebin stood in the doorway looking at Dennis's pinched little face and thought: "Perhaps this is the last time I shall see him alive. If only he gets better, I'll take him for a holiday, somewhere where there are lots of boats and books; the poor little chap likes reading." He stood there by the door gently swaying on his toes for a few minutes and suddenly said: "Goodnight. Call me if I'm wanted," and went up his dark attic stairs. He was grateful for the darkness; for there were tears in his eyes.

The next visitor to Dennis's room was Emma. She started to creep away when she saw the doctor sitting so still by her brother's bed; but he noticed her drawn white face and tired, burning eyes and asked her to remain, talking to her in a soothing manner. He wondered if she had eaten that day and suggested to her that he was rather hungry and would be really grateful for a sandwich and coffee or even a boiled egg, "And perhaps you would be kind enough to eat with me because I've a real horror of eating alone."

"Alright, if you like." Emma agreed rather ungraciously as she trailed off to the kitchen; but when she returned sometime later to tell him that a meal was waiting in the morning-room she seemed much brighter, and he saw that she had washed her tear-

spoiled face and combed her hair. The nurse was now
in charge of Dennis; so they left the room together,
Emma gravely leading the way.

On the morning-room table two tall candles burnt,
shaded by red silk shades which made their food
faintly pink. The young doctor gazed at Emma in
wonder as he encouraged her to eat, and, when their
meal was finished, he asked her questions about the
life she led. He was astonished to learn that she had
only left the village on two occasions since she had
come to it as a young child. Once was to visit a dentist
in Birmingham, "It was years ago, when I was about
ten, but I remember it all so clearly. My grandmother
took me and we went part of the way by carriage; but
we also went in a train. I'd seen them of course, but
had only been in one once before when I was very
young, and it was wonderful. Everything was wonderful that day except that the dentist gassed me and I
was sick after; but that didn't last long. We had lunch
in the most enormous hotel, where you could hear the
trains as much as you wanted and there were waiters
and palm-trees wherever you looked. And the shops!
The windows were terrific, and I seem to remember
them being filled with great Chinese vases as big as
my grandmother and shining silks and jewels like
sparkling falling water with the sun on it, only it was
the light from electricity. There were some shops that
sold nothing but new books with bright paper covers.
I never knew new books had paper covers before. Oh,
and there were shops that only sold flowers, and one
that made sweets in the window, just masses of sticky

stuff whirling round on two pieces of metal, and it
never fell down. But the streets! They were so smooth
and dark when you could see the road — which
wasn't easy because they were simply covered in
traffic; no one even looked at cars, and there were so
many handsome cabs, and huge drays often drawn by
four horses, and the noise was sort of savage." She
suddenly paused for breath and then went on rather
primly, "Of course it was frightfully dark and dirty. I
suppose you have been there often."

"No, I've never been to Birmingham, but it sounds
a very fine place."

"Where do you live then, not London?"

"Yes, I live in London, in Kensington; but tell me
about the other time you left the village."

"Well, it's nothing much," she said flatly.

"Please tell me; I'd like to hear about it so much,"
he said almost pleadingly.

"It was only a cattle show at Leamington that my
father took me to once. We just went in a carriage
with the lawyer and his wife." And then her face lit
up again; "But you can't believe how big some of the
animals were, like giants; and some of the bulls' horns,
they were quite good enough to mount and hang in
someone's hall. There were horses too, and there was
a show for them and jumping, and the people who
rode them were so beautiful—the men as well as the
women. And the machinery is so fascinating when it's
all new and hasn't been left in fields for months on
end. And there were bees making honey in a glass hive
you could see right into. Have you ever seen a glass

hive? 'Observation' I believe they are called." Emma's brow suddenly puckered and she said reproachfully, "Hadn't you better go back to Dennis, now?"

Philip smiled as he replied, "Yes, I'd like to see him before I go. I have to visit the hospital as soon as Doctor Hatt takes over here."

They walked up the stairs together without speaking and, as they entered Dennis's room, he whimpered like a small puppy. Philip bent over him and gently lifted one eyelid and examined his eye. While he was taking his pulse Doctor Hatt arrived and apologised to Emma for letting himself into the house from the garden "to save disturbing anyone," he added. "And you should be in bed Emma. I assure you, if Dennis becomes worse, I will have you called immediately."

So Emma, who had not slept for two nights, went to her room slightly reassured, and, only partly undressing, she fell on her hard white bed and was almost immediately asleep. It was early morning when she awoke to hear voices on the landing and softly running feet. Outside the birds were all singing and twittering wildly as if there had been a great silence which had suddenly ended. Her door opened slightly, and the nurse's face appeared. When she saw Emma was awake she came into the room and said:

"Oh, my dear, your brother has just died. He suddenly became much worse and there was no time to call you."

CHAPTER XVI

I T WAS a small funeral, and Ebin and old Ives were the only mourners from Willoweed House. Ives had not expected Dennis to die and had not planned a wreath for him; but eventually he had made one of many marguerites very close together, and as he stood by the grave he worried in case it was too feminine for a boy.

"But you couldn't call him a boyish boy," he muttered to himself; and the vicar stopped reading the burial service and frowned. The two doctors stood together under one umbrella, and the rain poured down and the grave was gradually filling with water round the little coffin. Ebin noticed a dead shrew mouse by his feet and carefully manoeuvred it with his shoe until it fell in the grave. "It will keep him company," he thought. The vicar again stopped the service, glowered at the small object lying among the watery wreaths, and then ended the service with a prayer.

In the morning-room at Willoweed House the bereaved grandmother discussed her will with the lame Lawyer Williams. Sometimes she shouted at him in a threatening manner and then almost immediately she would whine that she was only a miserable old woman with no one to help her. This assumed pathetic whine was a recent affectation of hers and was very embarrassing and trying to those who came in contact with her.

"I can't last for ever," she almost shrieked. "What will become of my money when I die? And my good land all let out so advantageously. I can't leave it to that fool Ebin, he'll most likely sell it and fritter the money away in London." She paused and then went on more quietly, "Perhaps he isn't such a fool after all. I can't say why, but he has been different lately and seems to have got money from somewhere. But I don't want to leave him mine except perhaps a little annuity or something like that. He's just like his father —the same idiotic face and lazy ways. I've never liked either of them and frankly I was glad when my husband died and everything became mine after only putting up with him for three years. Ha! You are shocked, you old hypocrite."

The lawyer laughed nervously. His laugh was a sort of bleat out of one side of his mouth, and he tucked his face into his neck in the most extraordinary one-sided manner when he gave it — which was about once in every four minutes if he was with a difficult client.

After much shouting and wailing on Grandmother Willoweed's part and bleating from Lawyer Williams it was arranged that a new will should be drawn up leaving Ebin, Emma and Hattie an equal interest in her property until Emma had a son, who would inherit the entire property at the age of twenty-one, less three thousand pounds, which was to be divided between the previous beneficiaries.

"Of course this is entirely between ourselves, Williams. I can't have Emma rushing off to get married and leaving me a lonely old woman dependent on servants. I can't last much longer, but even if I do she will still be young in another ten or fifteen years."

As Williams was preparing to leave Ebin returned.

"I'm home, Mother, and completely drenched," he said dejectedly. "Oh, good afternoon, Williams. I didn't see you."

His round blue eyes darted to the papers the lawyer was stuffing in his brief case; but he could make nothing of them. As he climbed the stairs he pondered on the significance of Williams's visit and guessed that his mother must be making considerable changes to her will now Dennis had died. For years he had worried over his mother's will and wondered how much she was worth and how she would divide it. What had rankled most of all was the injustice of his father leaving his entire fortune to his wife and making no provision for his son at all. But now he suddenly realized he didn't care what she did with her money. It no longer interested him, and as far as he was concerned she could leave it to a home for starving horses. He almost hoped she would, for he had always liked horses. He suddenly felt light-hearted, as if a great weight had been lifted from him, and as he discarded his wet black clothes he threw them round his room, and when he saw his trousers hanging

pathetic and limp from the piano he suddenly started
to laugh.

Emma had been lying on her bed with her head
covered by a pillow to drown the sound of the tolling
funeral bell. When it ceased she suddenly remembered
Hattie, probably alone and bitterly unhappy somewhere, and she left her bed and went to search for her.
She passed the morning-room and heard her grandmother's voice and the lawyer's bleating laugh, and
guessed Hattie couldn't be there. She opened the
drawing-room door and mustiness came out. There
was Hattie sitting on a yellow rug in front of the
window, bent over an exercise book. She turned her
dark, tearstained face to Emma, who thought she
looked like a pansy that had been too much rained
upon.

"I've been writing a poem," she said, "but there are
only two lines and I don't think they rhyme." And she
read out loud—

"Two people were swimming in the sea
One was alive and the other dead. See."

Emma assured her it was a beautiful poem except
that it was trifle short; and, as they stood by the window, the sun suddenly shone for the first time that
day and the garden became brilliant and glistened.

"Look how enormous the hollyhocks have grown,"
cried Emma, "I've never known them so tall before."

"And look at the sunflowers," laughed Hattie,
"They really are like suns this year."

They opened the French windows and ran down
to the river, and their home-dyed black dresses looked

kind of greenish in the bright light. They stood on the landing-stage looking down into the water, which had become so clear that fish could be seen darting below the surface.

•   •   •   •

Days passed and the village slowly returned to normal and the last cases of ergot poisoning recovered. Cricket matches were again played in the field by the river with the little white pavilion perched on the side. The choir-boys had their annual outing with the brass band playing on the vicarage lawn; and the first field of corn was cut, with the usual slaughter of rabbits on the last evening. Plums were gathered in the orchards, and in small gardens enormous marrows were fattening for the coming Harvest Festival. But things were not normal for the Willoweeds — far from it. There had been a dreadful afternoon when Norah had given in her notice to Grandmother Willoweed.

"You see, I'm going to be married to Mr. Fig," she explained with pride.

"I don't see, and I don't like people saying 'you see' to me, and in any case I expect you have made a mistake. I shouldn't think anyone would want to marry a big lumping girl like you. I suppose you're in the family way, all you village girls are the same."

Norah flushed right down to the large mole shaped like Australia.

"I am not in the family way, madam, and I must say you have no call to say such things about me."

Then she remembered Eunice's shame and it seemed as if it was her own and tears came to her eyes.

"Ha! You are becoming quite brave now you are leaving; but if you think I shall keep your lazy sister on when you've gone you are very much mistaken."

"Oh, no ma'am, my sister is leaving too. She is going to work for the old ladies at Roary Court. They need help badly since Miss Nesta has been so ill."

"Good God! What a scheming pair you are. I shan't give her a reference!"

The old woman's voice rose and echoed round the red walls of the morning room.

"That is quite alright, madam. Miss Nesta said she had known Eunice so long it was unnecessary."

Grandmother Willoweed struggled to her feet and she shouted from shaking jaws.

"So you are all in league against me! I won't have it! *I won't have it, you ungrateful wretch!*"

She suddenly seized a chair and started beating the horrified Norah with it.

"Bloody scum! Bloody scum!" she yelled as she rained blows on the girl who had fallen to the ground and was cowering in a corner.

Emma heard the terrible noises that were going on from the garden, and she ran to the morning-room, calling to her father on her way. For a moment she stood at the open French window so disgusted and filled with terror she could not bring herself to go to Norah's assistance. But she overcame her feelings and rushed at her grandmother and tried to wrest the chair from her iron grip. To her immense relief her father seemed to appear from nowhere and suddenly slapped his mother's face. She cried out in indignation, dropped the chair and then sank to the floor in hysterics. Emma helped the battered Norah to her feet and led her to the door; and when it was opened, a startled Eunice was found shivering in the doorway. She led her weeping sister down the long stone passage leading to the kitchen. The spluttering and screaming old woman on the floor gradually recovered and demanded burnt feathers, and Emma rushed to the henpen and quickly returned with a handful, which were burnt under her grandmother's pinched red nose. The smell was frightful, partly because the feathers were far from clean; but she seemed to enjoy them, although she was suffering from an attack of hiccups. Her son brought her a glass of water; but she threw it across the room and muttered reproachfully, "You struck me; you struck your own mother!"

She would not accept her son's assistance up the stairs and Emma had to support her to her room, and when at last she was in her bed she asked for marigolds to be burnt in the fire grate.

"Burnt marigolds used to be used with great success in cases of miscarriage; but I feel they would do me good," she whined. So Emma went to the garden and returned with a great bunch of orange flowers, which were damp and refused to burn.

"Yes, they are used for mourning in Spain. The coffins are all strewn with them," the old woman said sleepily.

CHAPTER XVII

WITH THEIR wicker baskets under their arms Norah and Eunice ran away from Willoweed House. Eunice went to Roary Court, where she was petted and fussed over by the two old ladies and quite soon had taken the place in their hearts that had once been occupied by their dead goat. Norah returned to her father's cottage and prepared for her wedding, and to earn a little money worked in the dairy that belonged to the farm where her father worked. In the evening she would meet Fig on the bridge and they would walk through the fields to his cottage and work there until it was dark. They scrubbed and polished and painted and papered the walls, and were completely happy in their quiet and gentle ways.

At Willoweed House there was absolute confusion. The grandmother kept to her bed and Emma had to struggle with the great range, which was appallingly vicious and refused to stay alight. There was no hot water and usually only an oil stove to cook on, and that was not much use because no one knew how to cook. Hard-boiled eggs and burnt bacon appeared on

116

the table three times in one day, and Ives kept arriving at the kitchen door with baskets of vegetables and
fruit which no one knew how to cook. Potatoes turned
into an extraordinary watery white soup when Emma
boiled them, and the runner beans became dark yellow
and tasted of nothing. Hattie tried to help and did suc-
ceed in making a kind of burnt toffee that set like iron.
She boiled some coffee for over an hour, waiting for
the grounds to disappear; but they didn't and it just
became all cloudy and her grandmother said, "That's
a bitter brew, child. Are you trying to poison me?"

The stone kitchen floor became black and greasy
and, when Emma washed it, it refused to dry and
stayed in muddy patches which trod all over the rest
of the house. Ives tried to help and said he would
make something called a skip-and-jump pudding. It
turned out to be a rather dirty spotted dick, which
never became completely cooked, and even his ducks
looked unhappy after an evening meal of skip-and-
jump.

Ebin Willoweed kept away from the kitchen and
told Emma running the house would be an invaluable
experience for her. He complained bitterly about the
food, but said little about the lack of hot water because he felt rather guilty about the range, although
determined to have nothing to do with it. He thought:
"If I once start that sort of thing, who knows where it
might end? My hands will be ruined, and they will
expect me to take up the old lady's breakfast and God
knows what."

Then suddenly Ives produced a middle-aged niece.

She came from Norton-in-the-Marsh and had never
been seen in the village before. Her name was Constance, and she was a Roman Catholic, and twice a
week she rode away into the misty autumn morning
on her enormous iron bicycle to attend mass in
another village. On those days breakfast was an hour
late; but Grandmother Willoweed never said a word
because the memory of Emma's cooking was still too
strong. Constance's cooking was plain and whole-
some, and however often her mistress ordered soufflé,
fricassee of veal, or stuffed turbot, she had to be content with salt beef, Irish stew or boiled cod, and the
only consolation was that the butcher's and fish-
monger's bills were considerably reduced.

"But I don't want to save money on food," the old
woman wailed to her son. "There are so many other
ways one can save money, and I shall be dead soon and
have to go all through eternity without a single meal.
Do you know, I even dream about tasty little dishes
now and wake up to find I'm chewing the collar of my
nightdress. It's not right — and she even roasts the
ducks without sage and onion stuffing."

"Well for heaven's sake, Mother, don't complain
and upset her. We can't return to Emma's cooking,
and at least she does keep the house reasonably clean
without any outside help."

"Yes, that is true, and I like to save on labour. I
think we could shut up the drawing-room and perhaps
just open it once a year — on my birthday, for the
whist drive. And then there is Dennis's room. That
won't be needed any more and may just as well be

closed . . . Good God!" She suddenly leapt from her chair, "I shall have to send for that fool Williams again!" She had just recollected that she had forgotten to bequeath Willoweed House in her will. How could she have forgotten her beautiful house standing in its four acres of well stocked gardens? She hurried from the room to write the lawyer an urgent note demanding his presence the following day.

Emma delivered the note. She pushed it through the letter-box of the ugly yellow and red brick house where the lawyer lived with his wife and daughter. As she hurried down the steps she thought she heard someone tapping a window; but she fled away because she did not want to be enclosed in the stale drawing-room with its beaded curtains and anaemic inhabitants. As she left the house she saw Doctor Hatt's enormous car, as yellow as a crow's foot, coming towards her, driven by Philip Andrew. He offered to drive her home. But, although she longed to accept, she connected Philip with Dennis's death, although he hadn't actually been there when he died, and she turned away and said she'd rather walk. Eventually he persuaded her to get into the car, and they roared through the village street and Emma was sorry to see the dark gates of Willoweed House leering at her between the pine trees. As he helped her from the car, he asked if she liked motoring.

"Oh yes, it's heavenly!" she said breathlessly as she smoothed her hair with her hands.

"Well, tomorrow is my last day here. Would you like to come for a drive? I'm sure Doctor Hatt would lend me the car."

"I don't think I could do that. My grandmother would never let me." She turned away, her face puckered by a worried frown.

"But need your grandmother know?"

"She'd know, I'm sure she would," Emma muttered.

It was the young doctor who looked worried now.

"It's my last day, Emma, and I've been wanting to see you so much; but didn't like to call and be a nuisance when you were so unhappy. I've seen you in the distance and on the river, but, when I try to catch you, you always disappear. Isn't there some way I can see you tomorrow?"

"Well," she said slowly. Then turning away she said over her shoulder, "I may be on the river tomorrow afternoon and, if you were on the bank walking or something, you would see me, wouldn't you?"

She reached the gate, fumbled with the handle and disappeared without looking back. Then she rushed into the house and managed to reach the bootroom window in time to see the big car start down the village street, changing colour as she saw it through different panes of glass. "But I like it best yellow," she thought as she walked upstairs swinging her little hat by its elastic.

On the landing she met a desperate Hattie sitting outside Dennis's bedroom door.

"They have locked it up. Oh, Emma, they have locked his door, and every day I go in there and look after his things. There is Dennis's grass he planted in a little bowl; he used to cut it with scissors and I've been looking after it for him. Do get the key. I can't bear his things all locked away for ever."

Emma felt guilty. How could she have felt happy so soon after her brother's death? Why, she had almost been flirting. She ran to Hattie and put her arm round her.

"Dear Hattie, of course we will have the door unlocked, and you shall have all his things and look after them for ever and ever, if that is what you want."

And together they went to their grandmother to plead for the key, which to their surprise was handed over without much comment.

"I can't think why you plague me with these things when I have so much to worry me. Here's the wretched key. Now go away, please!"

So they went to their dead brother's room. Already it smelt damp and unused, and the small black iron bed looked flat and lonely all stripped of its clothes. Seeing his bed like that seemed to make it more definite that Dennis would never come back any more, and the sisters sat on the window-sill and cried together.

Upstairs their father walked up and down the worn, turkey-patterned carpet which covered his attic floor. The carpet had been worn away by his bored pacings to and fro for frustrated years; but now he almost danced as he walked. He looked at the dreary room with new eyes and amusedly flicked the pom-pomed drapes on the mantlepiece as he passed. "Dear old room," he thought. "People like Doctor

Hatt can laugh at it, but it's been my only refuge from
that old tyrant downstairs for years. I shall lock it up
when I go; I don't want her prying about up here.
There is very little I shall want to take with me—just
a few books perhaps, and the typewriter. No, I shall
buy a new one, the very latest thing, with gadgets all
over it that I'll never be able to use." He wandered
across the room to the old machine and read a half
typed letter.

27th August, 1911.   Willoweed House,
                                            Fishingford,
                                                Warwickshire.

Dear Sirs,
        I have great pleasure in accepting your offer
of a permanent post on the *Daily Courier*.
        I agree to the salary and conditions you state
in your letter of the 25th ult. and would be free
to start work on the date you mention.

He picked up the letter from the *Daily Courier*
which was lying open on the table. He re-read it
although he knew every word by heart and then replaced it, still open, on the table. Oh, wonderful letter,
to set him free after all these years! The old libel case
which had lost him his position and which had ruined
his half-hearted efforts to find other journalistic work
was now forgotten. His ten years of exile were over,
and he was free to return to the work he had enjoyed
so much. He wondered if it would appeal to him quite
as much now he was ten years older and if he would
be able to concentrate on his work and keep it lively
and amusing. But of course he would. It was the kind

of thing he could have done on his head in the old days: just a gossip column twice a week, and the odd book review. But it would lead to other things. He would soon be back where he had been when disaster had almost drowned him. What a fool he had been to let it overwhelm him so completely! Then he remembered how his wife had turned from him, and the mystery of Hattie's birth. That, on the top of the other, was enough to shatter any man. And then there was his mother, that arch-viper. "My God, I shall be glad to be free of her!" he thought. Then he almost panicked. Suppose she became ill or had a stroke, could he leave her then? He made up his mind that even if his mother was dying he wouldn't delay his departure by one day. Emma could stay at home and look after her if necessary; but whatever happened he was going to escape at last. "As soon as the contract is signed I'll tell her and leave before she can stage something frightful, as no doubt she will," he decided as he picked up the letter from the *Courier* to read again.

EMMA EYED her rusty black dress with distaste. "What a thing to wear on the river!" she thought with disgust. Perhaps it would rain and he wouldn't be walking by the river after all. She looked up at the sky, which was grey but very high, and decided it was unlikely to rain that afternoon; and she was not sure if she was pleased or sorry. As she walked towards the river she hoped that Hattie would not guess her intention and ask to come too. Then she saw Hattie had taken away Dennis's boats from the little harbour they had made in the roots of a willow tree, and wondered if she was crying over them in her room. As she stood on the stone steps that led to the water she saw her sister sitting under a pear tree eating fruit and cleaning the boats with scouring powder. She seemed comparatively happy; so Emma returned to the river, selected the brightest cushions from the boathouse, flung them into the canoe and swiftly paddled away. She never felt really safe from her grandmother until she had passed the long garden belonging to Willoweed House. Sometimes a fierce, nasal voice had called

from behind an elm tree and she had been forced to
return; but to-day she was fortunate because her
grandmother was sitting in the morning room waiting for Lawyer Williams's visit.

She paddled past the pleasure gardens, lonely and
deserted as they had been all the summer. Since the
bread madness few day trippers had dared to come.
The motionless swings and silent iron tables with
their peeling paint passed from her view; and the
banks became higher, sharply outlined against the
sky and sometimes decorated by gently swaying
willow-herb, or dry, dead sorrel.

The young doctor was standing in a little bay
watching a shoal of minnows in the shallow water.
His panama hat was rolled up in his hand like a scroll,
and he waved it when he saw Emma appearing round
a bend in the river. She smiled nervously as she turned
the boat into the shallow little bay, and she silently
prayed "Please God, let him like me and don't let me
be disappointed!"

They spent the afternoon under some willow trees,
and when they left their kind protection they were so
much in love they paddled the boat for about a mile
down the river before they noticed they were moving
in the wrong direction. When they parted on the
banks of the Big Meadow, it had been arranged that
Philip would call at Willoweed House the following
morning before he left for London.

"You're so young, Emma, I must ask your father's
permission before we can become engaged."

"But surely it's Grandmother's permission you

should ask?" Emma could not imagine anyone asking her father's consent even in a small matter, and to ask permission to marry seemed fantastic.

"We all belong to Grandmother. Everything belongs to her."

"No, Emma, it's your father I must ask, and I'm glad it is so. I should very much dislike an interview with your grandmother!"

They both laughed and Emma said:

"Do you think she is looking at us from her bedroom window with her binoculars? You know, she often does!"

And she laughed again.

"Oh, I'm so happy, it makes me keep laughing! I didn't know being in love made you laugh. I thought it would make me feel rather solemn and kind of holy; but perhaps that will come after."

Then they parted, and Philip stood on the bank watching Emma moor the canoe. She stood on the landing stage for a moment looking across the water, and then she walked away under a dark ivy arch towards the house.

    *   *   *   *

The next day Ebin Willoweed's contract from the *Courier* arrived. The family, with the exception of his mother, were in the midst of breakfast when Constance brought in the letters. For the last week, to everyone's surprise, Ebin had appeared at breakfast each morning, shaved and neatly dressed and stiffly collared. He opened the contract with shaking hands and there it was, all signed and official. He jumped up

from the table. He hoped one of the girls would cry,
"What is it, father?" and he would say, "Pack your
bags; we are leaving for London tomorrow!" But
Emma looked out of the French windows with a
dreamy expression on her face and Hattie was engaged
in floating her egg in a sea of bacon fat. "How dreadful
to be so lonely! There is no one to share one's happiness with when it does come," he thought, as he rushed
from the room.

"Poor father, it doesn't suit him getting up early,"
said Hattie as she cut into her congealed egg.

Ebin stood in the hall gnawing his nails, and his
round eyes were blurred with tears. He rocked gently
as he stood in the dark mustiness, and the brown
velvet curtains smelt as if dogs had lifted their legs,—
but there were no dogs. A toasted-looking straw hat
lying on a twisted black chair caught his eye, and in
a moment it was on his head and he had left the house
and was among the fir trees and ferns and dark stones
in the front garden. The village street was in a flood
of light, shimmering with morning radiance in con-
trast to the darkness he had left. "I'll go and see old
Hatt," he thought. "He'll be interested, and really
pleased that things are going my way at last." He
tripped into the sun, and the village women as they
beat their mats exchanged remarks about him as he
passed.

The young doctor was just finishing his breakfast
when the elderly housekeeper showed Ebin Willoweed into the dining-room. Surprised, he put down
his cup of coffee and felt slightly unwell. It's one thing

to ask a man for the hand of his daughter with a carefully prepared speech; but to have him arriving in a storming rage in the middle of breakfast is rather shattering. Why on earth had Emma told him already? But Emma was so timid he must have found out in some other way—from his awful mother perhaps.

Ebin was disappointed not to see his friend in the room, and grunted:

"Morning, where's Doctor Hatt?"

"Oh, er, as a matter of fact he has just left on a case. Won't you have some coffee — er — now you are here?"

"Coffee? No thanks. I may as well go if Hatt isn't here."

"Oh, please don't go," Philip said as he stood up. "I know this must be a shock to you; but can't we discuss it in a friendly way? After all, its nothing to do with Doctor Hatt, although I must admit I did tell him about it last night and he seemed to think it was quite a good thing, although Emma is such a child for her age. I'm quite ready to wait a year or even more if you think it necessary." He suddenly noticed Ebin's amazed expression.

"I say, you do know what I'm talking about, don't you?"

"Can't say I do really." Ebin wrinkled his brow. "You don't mean you want to marry Emma? You hardly know the girl, do you?"

Then Philip poured out his hopes and feelings for Emma until the room seemed to be filled with beautiful thoughts, promises and love.

When he had finished Ebin said, "Well, if that's the way you feel about her, you had better get married; but I had been hoping she would stay at Willoweed House and look after her grandmother. I'm shortly leaving for London, returning to my old paper, you know, and I thought I'd take Hattie with me for company and she would have more chance there. Plenty of schools and friends and that sort of thing. Still, if you don't mind waiting for Emma for a bit, she could stay with her grandmother for the time being."

"I think it would be a terrible thing to leave Emma alone with her grandmother. Poor child, she needs some life and gaiety. She has missed so much and knows so little. I was going to suggest that she lived with my mother for about a year before we married."

"But would your mother want her?"

Ebin was amazed that anyone could want Emma, whom he had always regarded as painfully shy and humourless, although good-looking in a melancholy way. He had often called her "a damn depressing girl."

"Oh yes, my mother would be delighted to have her. You see she is a widow and rather lonely since I left home to live in the hospital. My elder brother is a soldier and abroad most of the time."

"Oh, well, you seem to have settled it between yourselves; but you will have to tell my mother — I can't do it. There will be hell to pay when she knows I'm leaving and taking Hattie. You had better come back with me now as you are leaving today. I only wish you could have waited a day or two until I'd gone."

As they walked down the village street they were stopped by the vicar, who was pushing his bicycle and looking very Chinese indeed.

"Oh, Mr. Willoweed, you are just the man I want to see. I've a puncture."

"Good God, you don't think I'm going to mend it, do you?" Ebin exclaimed crossly.

"Oh, no, it was nothing like that. We are having a thanksgiving service next Sunday. The last of the sufferers from the bread poisoning will be out of hospital by then, and I feel we should thank God that this dreadful infliction has been lifted from the village."

The little yellow man looked so pathetic Ebin stifled the words that came to his lips: "What have I to be thankful for now my only son is dead?" and substituted "I'm so sorry I shan't be here"; but he couldn't help adding, "You had better ask my mother, I'm sure she would love to come."

The little man looked worried.

"You think I should ask her, do you? Perhaps you would mention it to her, and I'll drop her a line. Yes, I'll drop her a line."

He started to push his bicycle, and then stopped and said in a depressed voice, "I'm very surprised to learn that Old Ives is going over to Rome—very surprised," and he trundled away.

"I don't know what the old fool means," Ebin remarked as he walked towards Willoweed House.

As soon as they entered the hall they were pounced upon by Grandmother Willoweed.

"There you are! Am I always to be left alone with

Papists?"

"Here's Doctor Andrew come to see you Mother. He isn't a Papist."

"I don't care what he is. Neither do I want to see him. Go away, young man. I want to talk to my son!"

Philip had come in contact with the old lady several times during Dennis's illness; so he was not disconcerted. He exchanged an amused glance with Ebin and hurried towards the garden in the hope of finding Emma.

"Now Ebin, I want to talk to you. Come in to the morning-room!"

"As a matter of fact, Mother, I want to talk to you," he said as he opened the door for her to enter the bright red room with the sun streaming through the closed windows.

"It's like a furnace in here, Mother."

"Perhaps that is just as well as it appears that when I die I'm going to Hell. Yes, Ebin, Ives has been in this morning and informed me that he is becoming a Catholic and is already having something called instruction from Father Kendall over at Shalford. He also informs me that he is going to die in a State of Grace and he doesn't care to think of the state I shall die in. It seems I shall be lucky to get to Purgatory—but most likely shall lie quite forgotten in Hell. But that is not all. He wants to take two afternoons off every week for this instruction! As if anyone could instruct an old fool of his age!"

"Mother, I want to tell you something—" Ebin interrupted.

"I don't want to hear it," the old lady answered as she tried to leave the room, knowing that something unpleasant was coming.

Ebin stood by the door and shouted, "I want to tell you, Mother, that I am returning to my old paper and have already signed a contract to do so. I shall be leaving tomorrow or the next day at the latest, and shall take Hattie with me!"

"Oh, the ingratitude!" she screamed. Then her face started to twitch, and she whispered. "Now you have a little money you want to leave me, after I've sheltered you and your children all these years. Well, go if you will—but you can't take Hattie."

"Oh God, how I hate all the unpleasantness!" Ebin thought as he hung on to the doorhandle with both hands.

"Hattie must come with me. She needs a school and friends of her own age now Dennis has gone. You must see this is no life for her."

"How can you say that? It's a wonderful life for a girl to live in this beautiful house and large garden. And think of the money I shall leave her!" Then pleadingly. "Ebin, I'll get her a governess if you leave her with me—and a pony. She'd love a pony; and, although I don't care for dogs, she could have a dog as well."

"It's very kind of you Mother, to think of all these things; but Hattie is leaving with me, and that's definite. I'm sorry, but there it is!"

He opened the door with a sudden twist of his hands and was gone, leaving his mother amazed and alone facing the brown door. Her jaw trembled. "They defy me now in my own house. How has it happened that they can defy me like this?" she muttered as she left the room. In the dining-room she sipped a glass of port; but it gave her no comfort.

Philip and Emma were on the river path with their arms entwined when Ebin found and disturbed them.

"Hallo, hallo," he said with rather an awful, forced heartiness. "Well, I've told the old lady I'm going and taking Hattie too, and it really passed off better than I expected. You know, I quite thought she'd go off her rocker or something, like her Aunty Kate, who suddenly went crackers in Rochester Cathedral of all places! It created a scandal at the time, and she had to be shut up for quite a while."

"Father, you are not going to leave me alone with Grandmother, are you?" Emma said reproachfully.

"Well, I thought it wouldn't be such a shock for her if you stayed on a bit. Anyway you are going to visit Philip's mother, aren't you? So you had better wait here until the invitation comes. And then there will be your clothes to get ready."

Philip interrupted rather impatiently: "There will be no need for Emma to worry about clothes. My mother will see to all that. She will enjoy it, and there will be the trousseau to see to as well. That will keep you busy, Emma."

The idea of a trousseau had never entered Emma's head, and she was delighted with the prospect. Also there was to be a ring—'an emerald, I think, to go with your hair.' She was in a dream of happiness and

hardly listened to her lover and father arguing about
when she was to leave Willoweed House. Philip was
determined that she should leave with her father and
sister, and eventually it was agreed that it should be
so. They would all three be at Brown's Hotel on the
following Friday — in three days' time. And Philip
went away content.

He had already written to his mother about Emma;
but he had not yet told her about his engagement or
that Emma was to be her guest for some months. He
knew his mother would welcome the girl to the small
South Kensington house where she lived alone except
for her maid. She was a warm hearted, rolypoly of a
woman, intensely interested in people and (super-
ficially) in art and literature. She would be enchanted
with the idea of educating Emma and watching her
surprised reactions to the most ordinary occurrences
and pleasures. It would be like entertaining someone
from another planet. He rather worried how she
would take the surprise of the dark-skinned Hattie;
but he still had three days to prepare her, and he
thought perhaps a long talk about Gauguin would be
quite a good idea.

CHAPTER XIX

E ACH DAY had been more stormy than the last. Grandmother Willoweed had raved and moaned and even torn her hair, although she was already rather short of it. Each day had been black with despair, and no one had dared tell her of Emma's engagement. Ebin's one terror was that his mother would collapse with a heart attack or sudden stroke, and that at the last minute they would not be able to leave; but so far, although she frequently vowed she was dying and kept pressing her hand to her heart and saying, "Feel my heart," her health seemed to be bearing up fairly well.

Emma had secretly prepared Hattie's and her own meagre clothes, and now they were packed in two black arc-shaped trunks. As Ives and Constance had tried to smuggle them down the back stairs, their mistress's sinister old figure had appeared on the landing and she had attacked the trunks with a great black umbrella. Ives and his niece had dropped them and run to the safety of the kitchen; but one of the trunks had over-balanced and crashed down the stairs, and

would have crushed them if it hadn't become entangled in the banisters. And there it stayed right
across the back stairs all day and far into the night
until vibrating snores issued from under Grandmother
Willoweeds' door and her son knew it was safe to saw
the banisters and release the imprisoned trunk.

On Thursday—the last day—she refused to get up,
and lay in bed all morning saying she was dying. No
one took any notice; so she decided to get up, muttering to her self while she dressed: "This cruelty and ingratitude is unbearable." As she was adjusting her truss
she saw Ebin pass beneath her window and hurled it
at him. Her aim was good, and Ebin suddenly found
he was wearing a sordid crown which he flung off in
disgust. And so it went on all day. Plates were thrown
across the luncheon table and a tortoise through a window. Lawyer Williams was sent for because she
wanted to change her will; but as soon as he arrived
he was dismissed because she felt too unwell to be
bothered with him. She poured out her wrongs to
Constance in the kitchen, and when the woman tried
to sympathise with her she was told she was an "in-
solent simpleton." Constance turned round on her and
said, "Be quiet, you silly old woman! If you are not
careful you will be sent to the mad-house. I'm surprised they haven't sent you already!"

Grandmother Willoweed tottered from the kitchen
to the musty drawing-room, where she sat weeping
and chattering to herself. Through the French window
she saw Emma and Hattie run across the lawn towards
the shimmering river. Young and apparently happy,

they passed under the ivy arch and disappeared down the steps.

They went for a last row on the river. It had been their main source of pleasure for so many years, and every bend and backwater held some memory for them.

"There's the old willow tree that was struck by lightning!" Hattie exclaimed. "Do you remember we thought it would die, all split and charred as it was; but now it's covered in green leaves and quite healthy."

They came to a shady bay where everything looked very green.

"This is the place where we used to find so many fresh water mussels, and I always thought they were oysters," said Emma.

"Aren't they oysters?" said Hattie in surprise. "I've eaten them sometimes all raw. Emma, we will miss the river."

"I know. Although there is a river in London, it won't be the same; but we will become civilised, and that's something."

"Civilised! Aren't we civilised, now?"

"Oh, no," said Emma in a shocked voice, "we don't know how to behave and are dreadfully ignorant. Why, we haven't seen a mountain or a play, and we know nothing about art or clothes, and we can't even ride a bicycle, although I don't expect we will need that—the bicycle-riding—in London."

"But are there mountains there?"

"No, we won't see any in London."

"Well, I don't think we will get very civilised after all. Everything you mention doesn't seem to be there."

"Oh, don't be silly! There are lots of other things to see in London. The zoo for instance, and big hotels were everyone eats in evening dress. Philip's mother is going to educate me and show me how to dress. I expect it will be rather hard at first; but I shall be glad to learn."

Hattie suddenly started to cry, "I shall miss the river, Emma, and Dennis will be so lonely when we have gone. Who will look after his grave?"

Emma comforted her sister and told her she had arranged with Old Ives to look after the grave. "And he is to plant flowers all over it and make it quite beautiful."

"I'd love him to have one of those lovely round glass things with white flowers inside," Hattie said wistfully.

"Oh, no," said Emma in her new adult manner. "I believe they are considered dreadfully common, and they are never seen on good graves."

      *   *   *   *

While the girls were on the river, Doctor Hatt had come to say goodbye to his old friend and discuss Emma's engagement, which had his entire approval. They sat talking in Ebin's battered old room, which already had an air of doom about it.

"Well, I suppose this is the last time we will sit together in this funny old room," Ebin said as he rose from his chair and the broken springs zoomed on the floor. Doctor Hatt slowly got to his feet and tapped his pipe in the empty fireplace. He then said the words Ebin had been dreading.

"By the way, I'd better see your mother before I go. How is she taking all this?"

Ebin rocked backwards and forwards and said in a hearty voice: "Oh, mother's alright, a bit cut up you know, but really she has taken it much better than I expected. There is no need to see her; it might unsettle her and all that sort of thing."

"I think I'd better just have a glance at the old lady. Are you leaving her all alone except for Ives's niece?"

"Yes, but they get on like a house on fire. Its extraordinary, but they do. And of course we will often be coming home. She is quite happy about the whole thing really—well not exactly happy but pleased . . . quite pleased." ("God forgive me," he thought, "but I can't stay here any longer. If I don't make a stand now I'll never be free").

The doctor looked at him for a moment and then left the room, saying, "All the same, I'd like to see her; but don't bother to come down. I'll let myself out. Goodbye and the very best of luck."

Francis Hatt knocked at Grandmother Willoweed's bedroom door; but there was no reply. So he tried the morning-room; but she wasn't there either. Before looking in the garden he went to the seldom-used drawing-room; but there was again no reply to his knock. A snuffling noise caught his attention, and he slowly opened the door; and the first thing he saw was Grandmother Willoweed with her great bulk arranged

on a tiny upright chair. There she sat in the middle of
the room, crying and snuffling and rubbing her face
with her fists. When he spoke to her, she seemed
not to notice him; so he came quite close and put his
hand on her shoulder, which was trembling. The
dazed look left her face, and she recognised the doctor
and said in a shaking voice, "It's kind of you to come.
Do you know they are all leaving me like rats leaving
a sinking ship; but I'm not sinking, only dying — so
they could have waited."

Her face became loose and dazed again and she
muttered, "My three freak moles have got the moth,
although they are in a glass case, and the baker's wife
squashed my little cat; there is so little consideration
these days." Then she was silent except for the crying
and shaking.

Constance was summoned and ordered to put her
mistress to bed. It took the doctor and the maid a considerable time to get her upstairs, and then she
strongly objected to Constance parting her from her
complicated underclothes. At last she was in bed with
a hot water bottle, and the shivering and crying had
eased a little, and Doctor Hatt felt it was safe to leave
her.

He returned to Ebin's room, and Ebin's heart sank
as he heard his footsteps coming nearer and nearer
and up his attic stairs.

The door burst open and a furious Doctor Hatt
appeared.

"So your old mother's delighted to be left alone and
gets on with Constance like a house on fire! Well, all

I can say is, if you leave her in the state she is in, it will be murder, sheer murder."

"Oh," said Ebin weakly, "isn't she very well then?"

"No, she isn't, and you know it perfectly well. It's quite out of the question for you to leave tomorrow unless you want to kill the poor old thing. Surely you can stay a few days and make better arrangements for her. Isn't there any cousin or relative who can be engaged as companion?"

"No," said Ebin dejectedly. "She quarrelled with them years ago."

"I know," the doctor suddenly brightened, "you could take her with you. She could keep house and all that sort of thing; and you would be out most of the day, so she wouldn't be too much trouble."

"My mother come to London with me!" Ebin looked horrified. "I'm only going to London to get away from her. You know she has made my life hell for years, and I don't want to take that hell with me. You know what it's been like for me here; so for God's sake don't try to stop me escaping." There was a note of hysteria in his voice, and the doctor said soothingly, "Alright, alright, don't worry. Perhaps we will think of some solution in the morning."

Then he left, and Ebin, with his hopes of freedom almost shattered, stared out of the window at the dusk.

CHAPTER XX

THE PROBLEM of how to dispose of Grandmother
Willoweed was solved that night, and five days
later it was finally solved when she was buried in the
churchyard by the river. Her son respected her wishes,
and her body was conveyed to the churchyard by
boat. The boat was again all draped in black cloth, and
the fine oak coffin was groaning under the weight of
many magnificent wreaths; but above them all was
Ives's wreath of grey-green holly, hogswart and
thistles. At the last moment he had felt the dande-
lions looked cheap; so they had been replaced by
yellow helenium.

Hattie and Emma stood on the landing-stage and
watched the funeral boat slowly pass round the
island in the misty September sun. The church bell
was tolling a lament, and men upon the bridge took
off their hats in reverence as the boat drew near.

"Poor Grandmother," said Hattie, "I hope she is
comfortable in that beautiful box. It doesn't seem
large enough to me. Do you think they have folded
her up, Emma?"

When the burial was over, the people came to the
house for refreshment, and there was much black
upon the tenant farmers and their wives. They wanted
to stay for the reading of the will so that they would
know to whom they belonged; but Lawyer Williams
turned them away and told them they would be noti-
field in due course. As he read the complicated will,
his bleating laugh was heard above the words he read:
but in spite of this it became clear to his hearers that
Grandmother Willoweed had left a very large fortune, the interest of which her two granddaughters
and son were to enjoy until Emma had a son, and that
son became of age, when he would inherit everything
with the exception of three thousand pounds. Old Ives
was left two hundred pounds, which he immediately
decided to give to the Catholic Church, "because it
can't do me much good on this earth, but it might
make all the difference in the next world when the
Almighty God hears how generous I've been."

The guests left, and Ebin was alone with the two
girls, and they walked up and down one of the lawns
talking together. The evening sun fell in slanting rays
on their black clothes, and in the flower-beds great
curly-headed dahlias blazed away.

"Do you know, I really think I should stay on here
to manage things," Ebin said, eyeing Emma rather
nervously. She looked at her father in amazement.

"But I thought it was all arranged that you were
going to London and you'd signed that contract?"

"Well, I think I could get out of that, you know;
and I must put my daughter's welfare before my own

inclinations. You would like me to keep an eye on the property, wouldn't you, Emma?"

"Lawyer Williams and the executors will do that, won't they, father?"

"Of course, Lawyer Williams will do all he can— after all he's been well paid for it — but it's rather hard on the executors; they are supposed to do it as a labour of love, and I'd like to help them as much as possible."

"If you are not going to London, need I go Father? I'd much rather be here. I don't care as much about being civilized as Emma does. Anyway she's going to be married, and it's years before anyone will want to marry me."

"But Hattie — your school!" Emma said in a shocked voice.

"London isn't the only place with schools. There is a high school only about five miles away. They come and bathe in the river sometimes and all scream behind bushes while they dress. I could go there and scream behind bushes, too."

"Emma, I've suddenly realised that Hattie's and my income combined will be a very handsome one. We could run a car and there would be no problem about getting her to school,—and she could have a pony. I remember poor Mother saying she would like Hattie to have a pony. Oh yes, there was a dog as well. Hattie, you must have a dog. Do you know I think we could be very happy here. It's a pity you are getting married, Emma, or you could have stayed as well!"

.   .   .   .

But Emma went to London and married her young doctor and became completely civilised. In due course the son was born who was to inherit most of his great-grandmother's fortune. He was pushed round Kensington Gardens in the most modern of prams by a brown-clad veiled nurse, and when he grew older he was sometimes allowed to sail his boats in the Round Pond, although he had to be very careful not to get his feet or clothes wet. His mother became a model young wife and hostess, very much admired for her grave, quiet dignity and elegant, but restrained, manner of dressing. She did not visit her sister or father very often.

Hattie was truly happy at Willoweed House, and her father was as happy as his nature would allow him to be. Ebin drove his daughter to school in a glorious green-and-black-striped, fifty-horse-power, Sheffield Simplex, all upholstered in grey. On the back seat an enormous white poodle lay in all its extravagant beauty. The High School girls were so impressed with all this they hardly noticed Hattie's almost black face and, when it gradually dawned on them she was strangely dark, they christened her the A.P. (African Princess).

Ebin grew a dashing red beard, which gave him a rather nautical appearance, and after being several times mistaken for a sailor, he began to dress in a sailor's fashion. The villagers forgot he had never been to sea, and in time he came to be regarded by all as a retired sailor, until he became known as Old Captain Willoweed. Before this came about he actually purchased a small sailing boat. When there was not much wind he could be seen sailing with his daughter and heard shouting instructions in a hearty booming voice. Hattie did most of the sailing, completely disregarding his instructions; so they managed very well.

Old Ives lived for many years, outliving all his ducks. He spent much time in the coach house polishing the splendid car and singing hymns as he worked; but he sometimes worried in case he had made a mistake in giving his fortune to the Church: it seemed as if the time would never come when he would reap the benefit.

THE   END